REBEL HEART

LK FARLOW

Brianna —
Be a rebel!
♡ LKF

© 2018 by LK Farlow
All rights reserved.
Cover Design & Interior Formatting: Jersey Girl Design | Juliana Cabrera
Editing: Librum Artis Editorial Services | Gray Ink Editing

www.authorlkfarlow.com

No part of this publication may be reproduced, distributed, or transmitted in any form or by any means, including photocopying, recording, or other electronic or mechanical methods, without the prior written permission of the author, except in the case of brief quotations in a book review.

This is a work of fiction. Names, characters, businesses, places, events and incidents are either the products of the author's imagination or used in a fictitious manner. Any resemblance to actual persons, living or dead, or actual events is purely coincidental.

The author acknowledges the trademark status and trademark owners of various products referred to in this work of fiction, which have been used without permission. The publication/use of these trademarks is not authorized, associated with, or sponsored by the trademark owners.

"REBEL HEART HAS SPUNK UNLIKE ANYTHING
WE HAVE SEEN FROM LK FARLOW YET!"
- JOY, HEA NOVEL THOUGHTS

OTHER TITLES BY LK FARLOW

Southern Roots Series
Coming Up Roses
An Uphill Battle
Weather the Storm

To my Phoobs
Thank you for loving my Rebel Heart instead of trying to tame it.

CHAPTER ONE

AJ

No.

Such an amazing little word. Magical, really. Just two little letters, but when put together they're packed with so much power.

"No, I will not share my food with you." I say that one every time I go out with Stacia, my best and only true friend.

"No, you may not use my study guide." This one goes out to all the jocks in my classes. Seriously, taking notes isn't that hard—it requires nothing more than a pen, a piece of paper, and half a brain.

"No, you may not have my number." Might as well tattoo that one to my forehead, and at this point, what's one more piece of ink?

"No, I don't want to meet for drinks." Not now, not ever, stop asking, I typically add on silently…unless you're tall, dark, and handsome and know how to use the tools the good Lord gave you.

"No, I don't want to tell you about my tattoo. And no, you sure as shit can't touch it." That's right up there with feeling up baby bumps and bald heads.

And, now, I'm using my favorite two-letter word to tell my British Literature professor, "No, I will not tutor some jock so that he can maintain his eligibility."

"I'm not asking, AJ," Professor Doss informs me, staring at me over the rim of her turquoise cat-eye glasses.

"What do you mean you're not asking?"

"I'm telling. He needs the help, and you have the knowledge. You should know, more than anyone, not to judge a book by its cover." *Cue imaginary eye roll.* Yeah, yeah, with my vibrant tattoos, cotton candy colored hair, and overall bad attitude, I really shouldn't judge others. But, an athlete? *No thanks. I think I'd rather get my next tattoo in some dude's kitchen.*

"Telling? Why?" I ask, my patience wearing thin.

"Telling because we both know you have the time, and if you want a recommendation letter from me, this is what it's going to take to acquire one. Take it or leave it, your call."

Professor Doss's words cause me to wince, because dammit, she's got my arm twisted behind my back—metaphorically, of course. I don't just want her letter, I *need* it if I want a real shot at getting an internship with Booking Out—a not-for-profit childhood literacy program. She was a project kickstarter for them, and her opinion carries weight.

With a long, heavy sigh, I give Professor Doss a terse nod, causing her to break out into a bright, toothy smile. "Good choice. I'll give him your student email, and he'll be in contact."

"Yippie," I mutter, sounding as *un*enthused as possible.

Agitated, I quickly dash across campus toward the café to meet Stacia, hardly taking the time to notice the lush green grass lining the cobbled sidewalk or the gorgeous live oaks shading the path. Prewit U has a breathtaking campus chock-full of the Southern Mississippi charm that I tend to take for granted due to being a lifelong native. People—mostly out-of-towners—always ask how I like living in such a small town. I guess they think with me being *me* that I must feel stifled in such tiny town smackdab in the middle of the Bible Belt, but Cottonwood is a fairly open-minded place—you know, except for the old money assholes.

I breeze through the double doors fifteen minutes past the time we agreed on, and knowing Stacia, she's about to let me have it. I forego the order counter and make my way to our table in the far corner. "You're late," Stacia points out, just like I knew she would. Which is ironic, because swear to God, the girl will be late to her own funeral.

"Yup, sorry. Doss held me up," I explain, and she huffs out a breath that scatters her wispy black bangs.

"Ugh. What for?"

"Apparently if I want her letter of recommendation

I have to tutor some beefcake athlete."

Stacia blinks her big, brown doe eyes at me and straightens her septum ring before bursting out into raucous laughter. I glare at her, wholly unamused. "Oh my God, AJ. That's amazing."

"Check a dictionary. Amazing is *not* the word you're looking for."

"No, babe, it really is."

"How so?" I demand, stealing her iced latte from where it was resting on the table in front of her.

She snatches it back. "Get your own." Slowly, she gulps down several swallows before continuing. "And, it's amazing because it will provide endless entertainment for me."

"You're a bitch," I tell her, and she just laughs all the harder. "Whatevs. I'm out." I stand from the table and sling my crossbody over my shoulder.

"You know you love me!" Stacia yells dramatically as I walk away from our table. Glancing back at her, I shoot her a wink and carry on my way.

It's ten o'clock, and I'm deep into the paper I'm writing when the email notification on my laptop dings, alerting me to a new message. I click *save* on my paper and switch over to my web browser. My inbox shows one new message from a B. Larson.

From: B.Larson@PrewitU.edu

REBEL HEART

> To: A.Adams2@PrewitU.edu
> Subject: Tutoring
> Hey AJ,
> Professor Doss gave me your email address and told me to reach out to you about tutoring. I'm available on Tuesdays and Thursdays at five. Meet me at the library.
> -Brock

No, no, no, no. There's that word again. Except this time, it's a prayer. A down-on-my-knees-begging-I'm-wrong kind of prayer. *Brock fucking Larson.* The bane of my existence since age twelve. I blink at my screen in a daze. *It can't be.* I reread the email at least six more times, desperately hoping for his name to magically change.

In a panic, I grab my phone and dial Stacia. She knows all about Brock and our stupid, sordid past—if you can even call it that. After all, she's been my best friend since he ditched me. She comes from old money just like me, only her parents are loving and supportive.

Like a good girl, she answers on the first ring. "Knew you still loved me, AJ."

"Always, but not the point. Brock Larson. Please, *please* tell me there are two Brock Larson's enrolled here."

"No can do, babe. Only one, why?" Her question is met with silence. I'm petrified that speaking it aloud will make it true—well, truer. Luckily, Stacia's a smart girl and figures it out all on her own. "Oh, no way. You've got to be kidding me."

"I wish I was."

"Sucks balls, AJ. That sucks balls."

"Donkey ones," I lament.

"You're just gonna have to put on your big girl panties and deal with it. This letter is more than worth dealing with his particular brand of BS."

I run my fingers through my bubblegum colored locks and sigh into the phone. "Ugh. You're right. Promise you'll help keep me sane?" I ask, all but begging.

"Duh. Now, go to sleep. Worry about tomorrow's problems tomorrow."

I disconnect the call and place my phone on its charging dock before scanning over his email once more. Only this time, my prior panic over *who* I'm tutoring is replaced with rage over the actual content of the email. How dare he just assume I'm free and willing to bend to his schedule. *Ugh.* That's so like him to be an arrogant little prick—like father, like son.

Pissed as hell, I shut down my laptop and place it on my nightstand. With one more long, drawn-out sigh, I let my head hit the pillow and drift to sleep imagining tearing him a new asshole on Tuesday when I see him.

CHAPTER TWO

BROCK

Look, Dad, I really have to go. I'm going to be late.

Per usual, when Dad hears something he doesn't like, he ignores it, and right now he doesn't like the thought of me deciding when to end our call. "How's your handicap?"

"Plus two," I mumble, tugging the ends of my slightly overgrown brown hair, dreading his response. After all, Everett Brantley Larson is banking on me to follow in his footsteps—or maybe it's that he plans on living vicariously through me. Either way, he's not going to like my answer, regardless of the fact that a plus two handicap, in most circles, is considered a good thing.

"Come again?" he demands, and I repeat myself, enunciating clearly this time around.

"I said plus two, Dad."

"Disgraceful. Absolutely disgraceful. When I was your age…forget it. Maybe I should bring on someone to coach you between team practices."

"But we practice five days a week!" I blurt out.

"Then we'll add him on the two days you don't," my

father grits out, his temper getting the better of him.

"Dad, I have a full course load, regular practice, the gym, homework, my volunteer hours, and my tutoring. I really don't think—"

"I don't recall asking your opinion, son. I've already emailed Coach Garza. I requested Saturday and Sunday mornings. Moving on, how's your GPA?"

Fuck. "Three-point-five," I tell him, hoping it's high enough to satisfy him, but I know it isn't.

"You know, I really expected more from you, Brock. Your mother is going to be so disappointed when I relay all of this to her." He clucks his tongue at me, and I roll my eyes, knowing my mom won't care even an iota. She's always been my biggest supporter and would fucking be proud of me even if I was a slacker with a C-average. These are things most parents would be proud of, but nothing less than perfect is enough for my dear old dad. "What class are you struggling with?"

"Lit, but I've already set up a tutor. In fact, I'm running late to—"

"I'll email your professor and make sure your tutor is the best of the best. I've got to run, son, talk later," he barks into the phone, like I haven't been trying to end the call for the last fifteen minutes.

I'm close to twenty minutes late when I make it to the library—I hope this AJ guy is still here, but I wouldn't blame him for bailing. Shit knows I would have. From the doorway, I scan the tables, looking for a familiar face from my lit class.

On my first sweep, I don't notice anyone I know. So, changing tactics, I begin looking for anyone who looks like a tutor. *Do tutors have a certain look?* I'm picturing thick glasses and a pocket protector, but once again, I come up empty. I'm about to turn and leave when the sensation of being watched rolls over me, making the hairs on my arms stand on end. I give the room one last sweeping glance and just about stumble when I see a set of brown eyes I'd know anywhere glaring daggers in my direction. The look she's aiming at me is damn near lethal. *Why in the hell is sweet little Abby Jane Adams mad at me?* Then again, Abby Jane isn't little anymore. Or sweet.

Once upon a time, those brown eyes were the highlight of my day—seeing them light up with laughter, watching her cheeks blossom pink. Her smile was brighter than the sun, and her laughter was sweeter than anything I'd ever known. Even as a kid, I knew there was something special about her, which is why it didn't bug me too much when our moms talked about us getting married when we were grown. Because, at age five, over mud pies, I decided Abby Jane would be my wife.

Turned out life had other plans. Middle school hit, I shot up by five inches, and suddenly girls thought I was cool. Abby Jane though, she was a late bloomer, and thanks to the glorious travesty that is grade school hierarchy…and me being a thirteen-year-old horndog…Abby Jane and I grew apart.

By high school, we hated each other. Well, she hated me. She was the antithesis of everything our families stood for. She was loud, opinionated, bossy, crude, and was always testing the limits, whereas I walked the straight and narrow. Her mother constantly asked why she couldn't just do as she was told, like I did, which didn't help matters between us.

Still, none of that explains why she's looking at me like she wishes she could roast me over an open flame.

Cocking my head to the right, I lift my brow at her in question, and she wastes no time marching right over to me. *How freaking weird.*

"How nice of you to *finally* show up, Larson," she barks at me, her eyes full of fire.

"Show up for what?" I ask.

"Tutoring, Jockstrap."

"Tutoring? You're my…oh, shit."

"Yeah, oh shit is about right. You're twenty-five minutes late now and I swear, if you ever show up even ten minutes late again, it will be our last session."

"Sure thing, Abby Jane." I bite back my smile. "Oh, and by the way, golfers don't wear jockstraps."

She sears me with her glare.

"So…are we going to…" I wave my hand over her already open textbook. Looks like me being late didn't stop her from getting started. Swear, you'd never peg her for the nerdy type, based on looks alone.

However, judging from the current look on Abby Jane's face, she's murdered me twenty times over in her head.

Slowly, she pivots in her chair so that she's fully facing me, and while I know I shouldn't, I can't help but rake my eyes down her body, from her bubblegum hair to her perky little B-cup tits covered in an old, faded Nirvana shirt that cuts off about an inch above her skintight leggings, revealing a delicious slice of skin, all the way down to her busted-up aqua Chuck Taylors. She may not be my type, but there's no denying Abby Jane is fine as fuck.

I'm still glued to that sliver of skin when something smacks me in the face. "Hey! Pervert!"

My eyes fly back to hers and then fall to the offending object that hit me—a pencil. *She threw a fucking pencil at me.* Smirking, I snatch it up from where it landed on the table and inspect it, pretending it's the most interesting thing I've ever seen. I run my thumb over the bite marks in the wood…a habit that seems to have followed her.

"I know you heard me," she bites out, her voice full of ire. "Brock!"

God, I love riling her up. Always have, though I didn't realize I missed doing it quite this much. "Yeah, I heard you, Bucky."

She falters, taken aback at the use of her old nickname, assigned not only because of her pencil chewing but also because of the buck teeth she sported until she got braces in fifth grade.

"You must *want* to fail this class."

Now it's me who's shell-shocked. "You wouldn't."

Abby Jane snaps her book shut and jams it into her bag. "Fucking try me." Swear to God, that girl needs Jesus—or some good dick. I watch as she storms out of the library, wondering how in the hell the two of us are going to survive an entire semester's worth of tutoring.

CHAPTER THREE

AJ

From the moment I peeled open my eyes this morning, I knew it was going to be a shit-tastic day. Why? Because it's Thursday—which means tutoring with Brock day—which is comparable to hell on earth. I would literally rather get a root canal with no numbing than deal with his immature ass.

Dramatic? Maybe.

Accurate? Fuck yes.

I tripped and face-planted getting out of bed this morning. My flat iron crapped out on me. The tip of my favorite eyeliner snapped off, with no sharpener in sight. The load of clothes I'd tossed in the dryer last night was still fucking damp and smelled like a dirty sock. And to top it all off, I knocked over my coffee can, spilling the grinds to the floor, thus rendering me coffee-less on today of all days. So, here I am, dressed in a pair of ripped-the-fuck-up leggings, a lace bralette, and a shirt with the sleeves and sides cut out, rushing out the door loaded down with my crossbody backpack, keys, and empty Thermos.

I trudge out to my sweet-as-shit matte black '69 Chevelle. No lie, this car is my baby. It was a gift from my grandpa—along with a generous trust—much to my parents' chagrin. When they realized I wasn't ever going to fit into the neat, well-mannered box they wanted to shove me into, they all but disowned me, going as far as shutting off my cell, canceling my credit card, kicking me out, and refusing to pay my tuition.

No lie. All because I wanted to go to Prewit U and double major in business and education, with a concentration in literacy, instead of following in the footsteps of the always-perfect Elenore Adams with an MRS degree. God, most people are proud of their children for having fucking goals. But my parents? They wanted me to become a luncheon-planning, tea-drinking housewife whose only ambition was to be able to fold a fucking fitted sheet.

Yeah, no thanks.

For obvious reasons, I was never daddy's little girl. Nah, the only thing that asshole and I have in common is our deep, coffee-colored eyes.

My grandpa—my dad's dad, mind you—is a whole 'nother story. I've *always* been a "grandpa's girl." From a young age, he's been my person. The one human on this earth who loved me unconditionally. So, when dear old mom and dad cut me off, Gramps stepped up something fierce. Knowing how much it pissed off the parental units? Simply a bonus.

A smile replaces my frown as I crank the ignition,

the deafening roar of engine sending a jolt of happiness through my body. There's nothing better than the sound of good, old-fashioned, American muscle. *Mmm, yes. Please.*

Even though I'm short on time, I make a pit stop at the campus coffee shop and order two large lattes: a hot one for now, and an iced one for later. Because something—mainly my impending tutoring session with Jockstrap—tells me it's gonna be a two-coffee kind of day.

Two classes later, and I was free. Well, free until five o'clock, when I had to meet *He Who Shall Not be Named*. That left me with a measly forty-five minutes to kill… just enough time to grab a bite to eat before heading to hell.

With a full belly and armed with my third coffee of the day, I whip my Chevelle into an open spot in the library parking lot, shocked as shit to see Brock pulling into the spot next to me.

We exit our vehicles—his a big, shiny, jacked-up truck…probably overcompensating for his small dick. I take him in as he swaggers toward me; his dark hair is pushed back from his face and his baby blue polo shirt—free of any wrinkles—pops against his tanned skin and makes his blue eyes impossibly bluer. I can't help but smirk when I see he's paired said polo with charcoal-colored sweatpants and leather slip-on boat shoes.

"Get dressed in the dark?" I ask, unable to help myself.

My body heats as he drags his eyes all over me—until his mouth opens, ruining the moment. "Pot, meet kettle."

Dammit. I totally opened myself up for that one, but still. His eyes lingered on the exposed skin from the cut-out sleeves of my shirt—*what the hell AJ? Since when do you want Brock Larson checking you out? Snap out of it!*

Brock moves in closer, running his knuckles over the hood of my car. "This looks just like your Gramps's old ride."

"That's because it is," I snap, marching toward the library.

Brock wastes no time and jogs to catch up. "Damn. You don't gotta be so snippy, Abby Jane."

Abruptly, I stop and spin to face him. "AJ," I clip out. "AJ. That's what I go by now. Two letters. Surely you can handle that."

His chiseled face splits into a wide grin. This asshole is grinning at my reprimand. "You'll always be Abby Jane to me."

CHAPTER FOUR

BROCK

The second the words pass my lips, Abby Janes looks ready to explode. Swear, if she were a cartoon character, smoke would be billowing from her ears. Using her momentary loss of focus, I stride past her, lightly checking her shoulder with mine. "You comin'?" I ask, just to rile her up a little more.

"I swear to fucking God," she hisses, following behind me.

For some reason, I don't feel like sharing her, so I lead us back to a secluded table that boasts only two chairs. Wasting no time, I make myself comfortable while she gawks at our seating arrangements.

"Any reason you passed the three open four-seater tables?"

"Just wanted to be alone with you," I croon, pushing her chair back from the table with my foot. "Now, have a seat; time's a-wastin'."

"You're lucky I need that damn recommendation letter."

Her words hang between us. Abby Jane blanches,

leading me to believe she didn't mean to divulge that little tidbit.

I hit her with my most boyish smile. "What letter would that be?"

Flexing her jaw, she pointedly ignores me. "Let's get started. We've already wasted fifteen minutes."

I'll let her off the hook *for now*…but she best believe I'm filing that shit away for a rainy day.

Much to my surprise, Abby Jane is as smart as a whip, and for the next forty minutes, we focus solely on the Brit Lit study guide laid out before us, only stopping when my cell phone begins ringing. I silence it without bothering to check who's calling.

But sure enough, it starts right back up. After ignoring the call, I turn off the ringer and lay it face down on the table. Right as I begin to find my groove, my damn phone begins vibrating against the wood, again and again, until finally, Abby Jane snaps. "Are you going to fucking answer that?"

"Wasn't planning on it."

"Why not?" she asks, scrunching up her nose, just like she always did as a kid when she didn't understand something.

"It's not anybody I wanna talk to," I say, hoping it'll close the subject.

Should have known better.

"Why?"

"Why do you care?" I counter, causing her to scoff.

"I don't."

"Mmmk. If you say so."

"I do fucking say so."

"Then it must be true." I steeple my fingers beneath my chin and held my gaze steady with hers.

"Jesus, your damn head is so big it's a miracle you can support its weight."

"Got something else big too—"

Abby Jane cuts me off with an upheld hand, just like I knew she would. "Don't even wanna hear about your teeny weenie."

I balk at her words. "Nothing teeny about it babe, but you do you."

She rolls her eyes. "Whatever."

We both attempt to get back into our study, but my phone starts up again, the vibration causing her highlighter to roll off of the table. "Seriously? Just answer it."

Knowing we won't get shit done if I don't, I snatch up my phone and swipe across my screen to answer. "What do you want, Amanda?"

What she means to be a breathy giggle comes through sounding so much like desperation, and I cringe for her. "Just to talk, Brocky."

"Don't wanna talk. We have nothing to talk about."

"Silly boy. We need to talk about rings."

I scrub a hand over my face before pushing back from the table. I stalk a few rows away and try once again to explain to this little psycho that we are not now and never will be an item, much less engaged. "Amanda.

Listen to me. We're not dating. We're not a couple. Please stop calling me."

She laughs like I've just told the most hilarious joke. "Oh, Brocky, don't be silly. I know you need to sow your oats before settling down. Just…hurry, okay?" Amanda doesn't give me the chance to respond before ending the call.

I make my way back to the table, muttering as I go. "Girl troubles?" Abby Jane asks, sounding sincere.

"Something like that." And really, I'm not lying. Amanda Burkett *is* a girl and she *is* trouble…she also happens to be the girl my parents plan for me to marry. Unfortunately, for every ounce of loathing I feel toward the situation, Amanda feels elation. She'd give anything to have my family's last name. Hell, it wouldn't surprise me if she already has monogrammed towels with it.

Abby Jane snorts out the cutest little laugh, melting away some of my frustration with Amanda. "Wanna talk about it?"

"Not for real."

For a second, she looks hurt, but she recovers quickly. *Like Abby Jane has feelings.* "Good, because I don't wanna hear about your latest hook-up."

I shoot her my most lecherous smile. "Your loss."

"Puh-lease," she splutters, and fuck if I'm not a tiny bit offended. She continues right on though, and I crumple up the sheet of paper in front of me, fisting it so hard my knuckles are white. "I'd probably need a map and a magnifying glass to find…"

REBEL HEART

Leaning across the small tabletop, I shove the wadded-up paper into her mouth, effectively silencing her. "Gonna stop you right there, Abby Jane, on two counts. One, you should know better than to speak about things you know nothing about, and two, I *know* at some point someone's taught you not to say anything if you have nothing nice to say."

Pissed as hell, Abby Jane attempts to chew my head off, but the paper's still in her mouth. "You muddafugger!" she yells, causing me to crack up. Only, my laughter's short-lived when a giant-ass spitball hits me square in the middle of my forehead.

I flash my eyes up to the pixie-sized she-devil seated across from me. "The fuck, Abby!"

"Gonna stop you there, Brock." Her voice sweet enough to give a dentist a cavity. "You should know the golden rule…do unto others and what not."

"Touché, Abs. Touché." Her cheeks pink to match her hair at the use of her childhood nickname, and not gonna lie, it does something to my gut to see her looking at me like that.

Actually, fuck that. I'm totally gonna lie. It doesn't do shit. I'm probably just hungry. Yeah, that's it. Thank God there's a Chipotle on the way home.

CHAPTER FIVE

AJ

T.G.I.F., motherfucker. After what feels like the longest week in the history of the universe, it's finally Friday, and I'm so damn ready to blow off some steam.

As Professor Doss finishes up her lecture on the themes of loyalty in *Beowulf*, I discreetly slip my phone from my bag and shoot a quick text to Stacia.

Me: Quixote's tonight?

Stacia: God, yes. Pick me up at 9?

Me: No. Come over and get ready with me.

Stacia: Done. See you at 7.

Grinning, I slip my phone back into my bag and tune back in just in time to hear Prof Doss dismiss us. After I slide my laptop back into my bag, I head down the stairs toward the front of the classroom, taking them two at a time. I'm almost to the door when Professor Doss hones in on me. "AJ. A minute please?"

So. Close.

"What's up?" I ask, walking over to the podium where's she's gathering her belongings.

"I just wanted an update on how things are going with Mr. Larson."

"They're going." I lift my right shoulder, the movement causing my bag to slip down my arm. She watches me like a hawk as I heft the strap up and over my head, securing it across my body.

"Going well?"

"Just going," I answer honestly.

"Let me remind you what's at stake, Miss Adams."

Slightly chagrined, I nod my head, and just like that, she dismisses me.

In true Stacia fashion, it's half past seven by the time she finally pounds on my door before letting herself in. She stumbles through the threshold with two bags draped across her chest and her makeup Caboodle in hand.

I arch my perfectly plucked and filled brow at her. "Why bother knocking if you're going to walk in like you own the place anyway?"

Stacia tilts her head to one side, and then to another, as if she's actually pondering an answer to my question before finally shrugging. "Habit, I guess. Now, let's get ready." She heads back toward my bathroom, and I trail behind her.

My apartment is another luxury Gramps' trust afforded me. Housed in an old factory, the complex consists of only six units. The minute I toured the unit

REBEL HEART

I'm in, I fell hard for the concrete floors, exposed brick, and high ceilings. It's located within walking distance from campus and downtown, and at just over twelve-hundred square feet, it's more than enough space for little old me—which probably explains why Stacia has so much stuff in my spare bedroom, even though she still lives at home.

While Stacia plugs her curling iron in at my double vanity, I make quick work of pulling a few outfit choices from my closet before joining her. I opt for a super messy updo that gives my hair that freshly-fucked look that boys go so crazy for. I compliment my hair with bedroom eyes and a glossy, nude lip—a stark contrast to Stacia's bold blue lipstick, but damn, she rocks it.

Back in my bedroom, I strip out of my lounge clothes and move in front of my mirror, holding up hangers in front of me. Eventually, I settle on a skintight, white bandage dress with spaghetti straps that ends just shy of mid-thigh, pairing it with a pair of over-the-knee heeled boots.

"Damn, girl," Stacia exclaims when she turns to look at me. I do a little twirl and then inspect her outfit of choice. The loose, black crop top ends just under her bust and she's paired it with a black leather miniskirt and royal blue peep-toe velvet pumps.

"Back atcha, bitch."

She shoots me a beaming smile before pulling a bag of Malibu from her bag. "Pre-game?"

"Always."

She uncaps the bottle and takes a healthy swig before passing it to me, where I follow suit. We pass the bottle back and forth two more times, and then we're out the door and on our way.

The line for Quixote's almost wraps around the building. "Is Cage working tonight?" I ask Stacia, referring to her cousin who works the door here.

"Girl, yes."

"Thank fuck. That line…"

"Is not for us." She finishes my sentence and we link arms, smiling as we bypass it.

"'Sup, Cage?" Stacia calls out as we approach her cousin, who has arms as wide as tree trunks.

He nods his head, acknowledging us as he slaps wristbands on and ushers us through.

The bass that was audible outside is now seeping into my skin, running through my veins, and rattling my bones. I fucking love it. Stacia grabs my hand and pulls me toward the dance floor, where a mass of bodies writhe, all set aglow by the flashing neon-colored lights.

We immediately lose ourselves in the rhythm, dancing around one another until a beefcake with six-inch liberty spikes winds his way behind Stacia, gripping her hips and rolling his body in sync with hers. I catch her eye to make sure she's open to his advances, and even though she prefers her men clean-cut, she shoots me a wink and a smile.

REBEL HEART

I don't mourn the loss of my dancing partner for long. Moments later, two big hands clasp my shoulders before trailing down my arms. Together, me and my mystery Casanova move to the pounding bass like we've been dancing together all our lives.

Then, the song changes to something sensual and moody, and he steps impossibly closer. The heat of his body sears mine and he grips my hips, holding me to him, moving behind me almost like he's moving *in* me. Our dance is the best foreplay of my life. It's almost as if he can anticipate my every move. I dip, he dips. I grind my ass into him and he grinds right back, his impressive erection lighting me on fire.

Ready to take this to the next level—also known as my apartment—I spin to face him. His scent invades my nostrils—a heady mix of sweat and Dolce and Gabbana Light Blue—and I swear I'm more drunk on him than the shots I took at home. I drag my eyes up his broad chest, admiring the way the black polo stretches across it, already fantasizing about his lips on mine, only to stop short when I land on my mystery man's face.

"What the fuck?" I screech, not caring one bit how crazy I sound.

Brock smirks at me. "Don't hate 'cause you liked it."

"As if!"

"Get real, Abby Jane. You were grinding on my dick like you wished we were naked in bed."

Shoving at his chest, I take a step back. "You fucking wish."

Brock doesn't bother with a reply. He just laughs deep and low before pivoting and heading toward the bar, where he posts up next to his older cousin, West. Turning away, I take a few deep, calming breaths. Even from across the room I can feel his eyes on me, heavy like a caress, and I'm determined not to show him just how affected I am.

Desperate for a drink, I head to the back bar and order a bottle of water, rolling it across the back of my neck before uncapping it and chugging it down. I'm about to set off in search of Stacia when a tall, sculpted Adonis approaches me. "Wanna dance?"

Playing coy, I pretend to ponder his request. Truly, I don't want to dance—not after Brock. But that just pisses me off, and I'm not about to let Jockstrap ruin my night, so I place my hand in Mr. Tall-and-Sexy's and follow him out to the middle of the dance floor.

He moves like he knows his way around the bedroom—and maybe even a pole—but I'm not complaining, and I'm certainly not comparing him to Brock. I'm also not searching out a certain black-polo-wearing jackass.

And my heart definitely doesn't drop when I see him dancing with a girl who looks like a real-life Barbie doll. Nope. Not at all.

My inner-denial is interrupted when my dance partner's hot breath fans across my cheek. "What's your name, gorgeous?"

Tilting my head back, my lips brush his neck as I

murmur "AJ." Our eyes catch, and I swear he's about to kiss me when suddenly he's yanked away from me.

"What the fuck?" he roars, his eyes pinned on the bane of my existence.

"The fuck is, she's only seventeen, it's past her bedtime, and her mother will gladly press charges against your jailbait-loving ass."

My eyes are wide with shock, and my blood feels like lava rushing through my veins. Oh-my-fuck, he *did not* just do that. "No! I'm not underage. Jesus Christ! I'm almost twenty-two!"

My Adonis glances from me to Brock, and that sabotaging asshole raises a brow as if to say, *of course she's gonna lie now, she's been caught*. Tall-and-Sexy lifts his hands out in front of him. "I-I didn't know." He slowly backs up before turning and hauling ass away from us.

"What is your prob—" Brock roughly grips my arm, though not hard enough to hurt, and practically drags me out of the club.

"My problem," he says through gritted teeth once we're outside, "is you."

"Me?" I yell, outraged. "I'm hard-fucking-pressed to see how *I'm* the problem. Only one of us here is a psycho-ass liar! You told him I was seventeen, yet I'm the problem? You've got a lot of nerve, asshole!"

He paces back and forth in front of me, tugging on the ends of his hair. "Yes. You! Jesus Christ Abby Jane!" His raised voice and lethal tone cause my nipples to pebble and that just pisses me off even more.

Even still, his words have my anger morphing to confusion. "I'm gonna need you to slow down and use your big boy words, Brock."

He halts in front of me, looking like he's about to blow a gasket. "You're in there grinding on some asshole, looking like your two seconds away from fucking him right there on the dance floor!"

I tilt my head to the left. *Is…is he jealous?* "And your point is?" I ask.

"My point," he whispers, a vulnerable look flashes across his face so fast I almost miss it. He starts again, his voice stronger. "My point is that you're embarrassing yourself, and I couldn't fucking bear to watch it."

I rear back as if he slapped me, shaking my head back and forth. "Wow."

"Abby Jane, I didn't…"

I'm about to tear him a new one when Stacia darts up to my side. "Cage told me Brock dragged you here. Are you okay?" she asks, inspecting me from head to toe before turning to glare at Brock.

"Yeah. Yeah, I'm fine."

"Abs," Brock says, his tone pleading.

I hold up a hand. "Save it. I have nothing to say to you. Unless it's Tuesday or Thursday at five, stay the fuck away from me."

Not giving him a chance to reply, I grab Stacia's hand and set off toward home.

CHAPTER SIX

BROCK

I watch on, shock and regret both swirling through me, as Abby Jane and Stacia stumble down the street. As pissed and confused as I am about how this night played out, I'm smart enough to know they're in no shape to walk home alone, so I trail behind, just close enough to keep an eye on them without alerting them to my presence.

I follow them all the way to an apartment building, where one of them must live. Once they're inside, I slip my phone from my pocket and fire off a text to West, asking him to come pick me up.

Not even five minutes later, his gunpowder gray Mercedes AMG-GT R is idling at the curb. Even though I'm pulling the door open, the jackass honks at me to hurry. "C'mon, get in!" he hollers.

"Are you drunk?" I ask.

"Nah. Only had half a beer. Now, let's go. I got someone waiting on me, if you catch my drift, and I need to drop your ass off quick-fast."

"Such a whore." I say the words with a smile.

West checks his mirrors before revving the engine and zooming out into the street. "Don't be jealous because I'm getting some tonight, and you'll only have your hand to keep your dick warm."

"How about you focus on the road and not my dick?"

"Wanna talk about you and little Abby Jane tonight instead?"

"Nah, not for real."

"You sure? You don't wanna talk about y'all went from practically fucking on the dance floor to fighting in the street?"

My tone is clipped as I reply. "Absolutely positive."

Ignoring the warning in my voice, West cackles like a goddamn hyena as he whips his car into the parking lot of the house I share with him. He's two years older than I am, making it the perfect living arrangement.

I exit his car, and he wastes no time throwing it into reverse. As he backs out, he lowers the window. "Don't bother waiting up!"

Once inside, the events of the night catch up to me. I trudge back to my room, stripping down to my boxers and collapsing down onto my bed. From start to finish, tonight was a total shitshow. The only highlight was feeling Abby Jane's plump ass brushing against my dick. *Fuuuuck*. In a flash, visions of her hot little body come rushing back.

I sink farther into my mattress, and like an ESPN slow-mo replay, I savor the memory of us dancing. Dragging my right hand down my abs, slipping it beneath the band of my boxers, I imagine us no longer on the dance floor, surrounded my other people, but in my bed, with her pink hair fanned out on my black fifteen-hundred thread count sheets as I rock into her hot, tight…*NO! Stop. I will not jerk it to thoughts of fucking Abby Jane.*

Pissed and horny, I jump up from my bed and stalk into my bathroom, cranking the shower as cold as it'll go. Stepping beneath the icy spray, I lather up my body wash, scrubbing away all thoughts of her and this backassward night.

Four days later and I'm still pissed about the Friday before. Somehow, she's managed to weasel her way under my skin. Then again, I've always had a soft spot for Abby Jane. Even after we drifted apart and she turned into some emo-goth freak, I never let the guys make fun of her. There's just something about her, and while I haven't thought about her much since we graduated high school, suddenly she's the only thing on my mind.

I'm like an addict. Over the weekend, I crept on her social media—even her fucking Pinterest account. I may as well turn in my man card, because *Jesus*.

Naturally, West caught me cyberstalking her fine ass, and he has no plans of letting me live it down anytime soon.

"Still hot for tutor?" he asks, slathering his bagel with cream cheese at the kitchen island.

"Fuck off," I mutter, moving around him to pour myself a cup of coffee.

"No can do, cuz. Never thought I'd see the day where Abby Jane had you wrapped around her little finger again."

"I'm not wrapped around shit."

"Maybe not, but I bet you wouldn't object to her luscious lips wrapped around your cock."

For some reason unknown to me, his words piss me off. I slam my mug down onto the counter, some of the steaming liquid sloshing over the rim. Crowding his space, I push him into the countertop, knocking his breakfast to the floor.

"What the fuck?" he bellows.

"Talk about her like that again, and I swear to God…"

"You'll what?" he sneers, getting right back up into my face. "Jesus, Brock. Do you even hear yourself? Do you hear how riled up you are over her?"

Feeling annoyed—though whether at his observation or my actual feelings, I'm unsure—I back up and mumble, "Not riled up."

"Whatever you gotta tell yourself. Have fun at tutoring tonight. Be sure to practice safe education." I reach out to smack him upside the head, but he skirts around me, snickering, leaving me to clean up his bagel from off the floor.

While I don't have actual classes on Tuesdays, I do have weight training for an hour in the morning—yes, golfers lift too—and I typically play thirty-six holes of golf with a guy or two from the team after lunch.

Today I'm out with Hayes, a freshman on the team, and we're on our second pass of the back nine when he pipes up. "So, last week I saw you at the library with some pink-haired girl covered in tatts."

In no mood to talk about her, especially to them, I scrub a hand over my face. "Your point?"

"Just wondering if she's single. She may not be the kind of girl you bring home to Mom, but she's damn sure the kind you want in the sheets."

Carefully, calmly, and quietly, I stow my driver back into my golf bag before pivoting to face him. With an eagle eye, I appraise him, taking stock. Scrawny, ginger, and barely five-ten, with his thin lips stretched into a pervy leer…I find him lacking, just like any self-respecting woman—especially Abby Jane—would. He lifts his fist to me, like I'm gonna bump it in support. Kid's got another thing coming.

"Talk about her—or any woman—like that in front of me again, and I swear to God, I'll tee my ball up on your dick." Seemingly, my threat has stunned Hayes into silence, and I use it to my advantage, hopping into the golf cart and leaving his ass to walk back.

Back at the clubhouse, I have just enough time to get showered and changed before heading to meet Abby Jane at the library. Just like last week, we pull up almost at the same time, and before I can even get down from my truck, she's glaring at me like she'd like to cut my nuts off and feed them to me.

CHAPTER SEVEN

AJ

I thought I was over the events of Friday night, but seeing Brock now, I know I'm not. In fact, I'm fuming. In addition to being a cock-blocking little weasel, he's also just like our parents—full of double standards and judging others like his shit doesn't stink.

We meet at the front of his truck, and he sighs. "You still mad?"

"Damn right I am." Without waiting for a reply, I march up the steps toward the huge oak door.

"Let it go, Abby Jane," he calls after me, and I spin to face him.

"Let it go? You want me to let it go?"

His eyes drop to my messy fishtail braid, where the ends brush the top of my T-shirt-covered left breast. "Yeah, Elsa, that'd be great."

I narrow my eyes him as he moves up the stairs toward me, stopping two below me so we're eye-to-eye. "Lemme ask you something Brock." He nods, waiting for me to continue. "Why was it okay for me to grind all over you but not that other guy?" Brock's eyes widen, and he sputters, unable to find a reply. I scoff. "Yeah, that's what I thought."

I turn and move to pull the door open when his hand lands on my shoulder, stopping me. "Abs, no. That's not…I don't…" I shrug out of his hold and enter the library, heading for a table right in the middle, surrounded by tons of other students, ensuring we won't be alone.

I situate myself on the far side of the four-seater table, stowing my bag in the seat next to me, relegating Brock to the other side of the table. He drops down into the chair across me with a huff, and I'm secretly pleased he's aggravated with me. He deserves it.

Wordlessly, I pull out my copy of *Beowulf* along with my laptop. Brock takes a hint and does the same. "If you need help, ask me. Otherwise, don't talk."

He shakes his head, looking a little sad. Though I'm sure that's just my imagination. "Whatever you say, Abs."

We've been working silently for about half an hour when the *ding* from my email interrupts me. I save my work in my Word document and toggle over my email account.

One new message from B.Larson.

The words practically flash on the page. *Why is he emailing me?* Nervously, I click on his message.

> From: B.Larson@PrewitU.edu
> To: A.Adams2@PrewitU.edu
> Subject: I'm Sorry

REBEL HEART

> Abs,
> Please don't stay mad. I know I acted like an ass, and truly, I'm sorry. I could list a million reasons as to why, but none of them will excuse my behavior.
> -Brock
> P.S.
> Do you think Beowulf went to heaven when he died?

As much as I don't want them to, his words make me smile. Even so, I'm not ready to talk to him out loud, so I crack my knuckles and hit *Reply*.

> From: A.Adams2@PrewitU.edu
> To: B.Larson@PrewitU.edu
> Re: I'm Sorry
> Brock,
> I guess I'll forgive you this once. But so help me God, if you ever act that way again, I'll castrate you.
> As for good old Beowulf, the author states that he sought the glory of the saints, so I'd say yeah, he did go to heaven.
> -AJ

Not even two minutes later, he replies.

> From: B.Larson@PrewitU.edu
> To: A.Adams2@PrewitU.edu
> Re: Re: I'm Sorry
> Damn you're smart, and while I'll never say it out loud, I'm glad you're my tutor.
> -Brock

I read his email twice, my cheeks blushing crimson. *Is he really glad I'm his tutor? Or is he just saying that?*

Thoughts race through my brain, one after another; I'm lost in them until he clears his throat.

"I mean it, Abs. I'm glad you're my tutor."

My teeth come down on my bottom lip, slowly rolling over it, and his eyes darken, roaming over my body as if he's cataloging every minute detail—from my scuffed-up shoes to my cotton candy flyaways. The hunger in his stare causes my body to remember the feel of him grinding behind me on the dance floor. *Gah! Snap out of it, AJ!*

"Thanks, Brock." I'm pleasantly surprised when my voice comes out nice and neutral, because good God, I was prepared for breathy and lust filled.

We fly through the rest of our session, working together to fill in the answers on our study guide. Brock impresses me with his knowledge, which makes me feel extra bitchy for assuming he was a dumb jock. Because really, he's anything but. It's obvious he works hard and is fucking smart. So, why *does* he need tutoring?

Wednesday passes by in a blur, and before I know it, Thursday is dawning, which means…tutoring with Brock tonight. Strangely though, I'm not feeling the usual annoyance or apprehension that comes with thinking of him. No, instead, there's a swoop low in my belly and tingling in my core. I squeeze my thighs together to alleviate the feeling, but it's useless.

My alarm blares, bringing the crazy, runaway train

that my thoughts have become to a halt. I silence the awful buzzing sound and force myself out of the warm confines of my bed and into the shower.

But there, under the hot spray, my thoughts turn back to my once friend turned arch-nemesis turned… tutee? But that doesn't seem like the right descriptor for him at all. Friend? No. Hell no. I one thousand percent wouldn't call us friends. Acquaintances, maybe?

Frustrated with myself, I finish up in the shower only to realize I spent way too much time trying to define my nonexistent relationship with Brock. *Jesus.* He doesn't even have to be present to drive me crazy.

Now pressed for time, I fly through getting ready, barely bothering to check what I'm throwing on. I bypass coffee entirely, flying out the door and into my car. My first class today is on the far side of campus and luck seems to be on my side, as I don't hit a single red light, and I manage to snag a primo parking space.

Clambering out of my car, I snatch my bag off my passenger seat and haul ass down the cobbled path toward my marketing class. Professor Boyce, while sweet as pie, is a stickler for punctuality, and has been known to lock the doors at five after.

A quick glance at the smartwatch on my wrist tells me class technically started two minutes ago, but the door is within sight and another student just walked in—*fuck yes,* I'm gonna make it!

Until…

My toe snags on the uneven sidewalk, and I'm

flying through the air, landing on my face and skidding to a stop, a pair of khaki-clad legs stopping my concrete slide.

"Damn, Abby Jane, I didn't expect you to go and fall for me like that. And so soon. What will people think?"

No. No. No. Luck, you fickle, prickly, two-timing bitch.

"Larson," I grit out, scooting back from him.

"You gonna stay down there, or…" He trails off, and I drag my eyes up to his, squinting to block out the sun, which is shining around him like a damn halo. He's smirking at me, like he's thinking of all the things he'd like me to do while I'm down here. *Ugh.*

"Yes, Brock. I'm gonna stay here, right here in this very spot, all day. How ever did you guess?"

He winks at me and taps two fingers to his temple. "My mom says I'm a smart cookie."

"So smart you need tutoring," I grumble under my breath, immediately regretting it. Especially when I see the hurt look on his face.

"Well, fuck you too, Abby Jane." He turns and walks away, leaving me in a heap of regret and late AF for class.

The rest of my day goes the same way. The arugula in my panini at lunch slipped out and landed on my shirt, bringing a healthy dose of garlic aioli with it, leaving me with an awesome white-ish jizz-looking stain on my black shirt.

My second and final class of the day—Early

REBEL HEART

Literacy—had a sub that was gung-ho on torturing all of us, and on top of all that, I've been simmering in my own guilt for how I treated Brock this morning.

I even spaced out during the second half of my EL class, dreaming up ways of how I could make it up to him, which totally backfired because the sub called me out for daydreaming. *Like, get a grip lady.*

Now, I'm loitering in the lobby of my apartment building, getting ready to head to the library, and the damn sky falls. Literally, it is pouring, and there's no way in hell I'm going out in that, especially after the day I've had.

But! This could be exactly what I need to make up my snotty behavior from this morning.

Inspired and inpatient, I skip the elevator and fly up the stairs to my apartment, where I retrieve my laptop from my bag and fire off an email to Brock, seeing as I don't have his number. *Note to self: Get Brock's number.*

Hurriedly, I type out an email to him asking him to come here tonight instead of the library. I include my address as well as my phone number and hope for the best.

CHAPTER EIGHT

BROCK

While I wish I could say Abby Jane's bullshit, snotty attitude didn't ruin my day but I can't, because it did. I mean, why's she gotta act like that? Why's she gotta act like I'm less than her because I need a tutor? Fuck. I don't even *need* a tutor so much as I need to make sure I set aside the time to do the work, and getting on someone else's time was the easiest way to do so.

You'd think someone who looks like her—more like a criminal than a scholar—would be a little less judgy. But, then again, given her silver-spoon upbringing, maybe some habits are hard to shake.

The sound of an incoming email breaks me from thoughts of Abby Jane, only the email is *from* her, so my mind circles right back. *I swear to God, if she's canceling…*

I click open her message, and my eyes almost pop out of their sockets. She's not canceling…not at all. She's inviting me to her house and giving me her number? I drop my phone onto my center console and pinch my arm, you know, just to make sure I haven't somehow been transported to the fucking twilight zone.

"Ouch, dammit!" Nope. Still here, in reality. Quickly I add her number to my contacts and fire off a text to her.

Brock: Headed your way, Abby Jane.

The message quickly moves from sent to delivered to read, but the little reply bubbles never pop up. As long as she knows I'm coming—God only knows how bitchy she'd be if I just showed up.

I glance back at the address she sent me and realize it's the apartment building she and Stacia walked to last weekend. So, sans GPS, I crank my truck and head her way.

Rain is pouring down in sheets by the time I guide my truck into a roadside parking spot about half a block down from Abby Jane's building. It's times like these I wish our small-ass town had parking garages. But, we don't, so hoofing in this damn tsunami is my only option. *Thanks, Mother Nature.*

From the second I open my door, rain is pelting me in the face like I've got a target on it. By the time I make it into the lobby, I'm sopping wet. I'm talking to-the-bone-wet. I sure as shit hope Abby Jane's found a more pleasant disposition, because if I listen to her bitch while I'm soaking wet…nah. Shit won't end well.

A short but miserable elevator ride later, I'm knocking on Abby Jane's door, slightly nervous for what may greet me on the other side. She flings the door open and stops short, her brown eyes flare wide, taking in the way my wet clothes cling to my body. It takes everything in me not to smirk when her gaze gets hung up on the way my T-shirt is molded to my abs like a second skin.

Finally, I clear my throat, and she rips her gaze away from my body and steps back to let me in. Once inside, the scent of lemon and garlic lingers in the air, and I turn to face her. "Abby Jane, did you cook for me?"

She ducks her head and nods. Well, I'll be damned.

From the aroma alone, I know it's going to be delicious, but I can't help but to push her buttons just a little. "And it's edible?"

"Yes, Jockstrap, it's edible." She rolls her eyes and smacks me on the chest, and once again her stare goes wide. "Oh my God! You're soaked!" She bites down on her juicy bottom lip, and without permission, visions of me sucking and nibbling on it invade my mind.

Stuck in a lusty haze, my words fail me. I nod and she steps a little closer, almost as if it's a subconscious kind of thing. "You must be freezing too. Fuck. Okay. Why don't you hop in the shower and warm up, and I'll toss your clothes in the dryer?"

"That'd be awesome." Abby Jane leads me through her apartment to her master bath, which surprises me. I was for sure expecting to use the guest bath.

Still nibbling on her lip, her gaze darts around the room. "Uh. I guess you can go ahead and get undressed"—I start to pull my shirt over my head—"Whoa! I didn't mean right this very second. Jesus! What I was trying to say is you can get undressed *after*

I step out, and if you leave your clothes near the door, I'll grab them and leave a towel for you to use."

Her nervousness makes me grin. I really like her a little nervous, and with that in mind, I finish removing my shirt, loving the way her hungry gaze feasts on all I've got going on: solid pecs, cut abs, and that vee around my hips that all the girls seem to love.

Not wanting to test my luck, or Abby Jane's hospitality, I amble over to her walk-in shower and turn on the water, fiddling with the temperature until I hear the door close. With her gone, I finish stripping and leave my wet clothes in a heap on her shiny concrete floor.

Stepping into the warm spray, I pull the glass door closed behind me. Nosiness gets the better of me, and I start flipping the tops of the various bottles lining up the little built-in shelf. So far, standard girl stuff, but the third bottle…some shit called Love Spell. *Fuuuuck.* It gives me pause. And by pause, I mean it gets me hard as a rock. Unable to help myself, I squeeze a dollop of the purple shower gel into my palm.

Rubbing my hands together, I lather it up and grip myself, guiding my hand up and down my hard length, imagining Abby Jane's hot mouth all the while. *I know this shit is wrong but damn. Maybe I'm okay with being wrong, because it sure as hell feels right.*

REBEL HEART

AJ

Flushed from Brock's peep show, I dash out of the bathroom the minute he turns his back toward me. In the safety of my kitchen, I fan my face, desperate to cool down. *Get a grip, girl. It's just a set of abs.* Apparently my traitorous body doesn't care that they belong to one of my least favorite people alive, because my God, I want to lick them. Go figure.

Once I've regained my composure, I check on the food. The sauce needs to be stirred and removed from the burner and the pasta strained. When all that is taken care of, I snag a fresh towel from the hall closet and crack the door to my bathroom open to exchange the towel for his clothes.

The bathroom's filled with steam, and it seeps out into my bedroom, along with a deep, throaty groan, followed by an "Oh, fuck," that sounds so dirty I worry I've stumbled onto a porno set.

On its own accord, my free hand nudges the door open a little more, and my eyes move straight to the shower door. While I can't see him entirely, fog and steam be damned, I can see enough to know that Brock Larson is in my shower masturbating.

Holy. Shitballs.

Not wanting to get caught ogling his goods, I drop the towel and flee, forgetting his clothes in the process *and* slamming the door. So much for being stealthy.

Great. Just great.

"Don't panic, AJ," I mutter to myself as I pace up and down the hallway. "Be cool. He'll never know." A few deep breaths later, I make my way into the kitchen to plate up our dinner. The "I'm Sorry" dinner I made for being a bitch is now, whether he knows it or not, to also apologize for inadvertently seeing him pleasure himself.

I'm carrying our plates to the table when I hear Brock pad into the dining area just off the kitchen. I look up and find him clad in only a fluffy white towel knotted around his waist, with his still sopping clothes in hand. "You forget something?" he asks, grinning like he knows all my dirty secrets.

"Oh. Oops." I force myself to look down at the tabletop, even though all I really want to do is count the divots and dips in his abdominals. While I may not have much willpower, I'm not desperate either. When the plates are safely on the table, I turn—eyes still on the ground, thank-you-very-much—and take his clothes from him. "Be right back! You can go ahead and eat." I make a mad dash for the laundry room, not giving him the time to reply.

I transfer my load of unfolded clothes to a basket and toss his in along with a lavender-scented dryer sheet, all the while mentally prepping myself to eat dinner next to a nearly naked Brock. When I join him at the table, I notice he's almost cleaned his plate. "Guess I'm edible after all?" *Oh, no.* "I…I mean I guess *it's*—"

Brock cuts me off, mumbling around a forkful of

pasta. "So damn good." I watch his Adam's apple bob as he swallows, wondering if his words have more meaning beneath the surface. "Who knew you could cook like this?"

Ah. There we go. Of course they don't. Which is fine. I don't want him to want me. I mean, hell, I don't even want him. No sweat off my back. Even still, I beam at his praise, pointing at my chest with my thumb. "I knew I could!"

"Well, feel free to feed me anytime, Abby Jane." He delivers the words with a Zac Effron-esque smolder, and is it just me, or is it hot in here? We finish eating and Brock stands from the table and grabs both of our plates. "I'll rinse these and then we can work on the rest of that study guide."

"Uh-huh. Sure." Although, I'm not really sure what I just agreed to. Nope, I'm too distracted by the way the muscles in his back bunch and flex. My eyes track him like a hunting dog following a deer as he moves through my apartment. To the kitchen and back. Past me and into the living room, scooping up his backpack as he goes. I watch with bated breath as he situates himself on the couch—my couch—with only a piece of terrycloth separating his skin from the leather.

"Abs, you coming?"

His words spur me into action, and I scramble over to the couch, throwing myself down onto the cushion next to him. The motion causes the towel to ride up, exposing more of his muscular thighs. "I can't fucking do this," I mutter under my breath as I dart back up from the couch.

"What are you doing?" I hear Brock holler after me, but I pay him no mind. That boy has got to put some damn clothes on before I lose what little bit of sanity I have left and climb him like a tree.

"Here!" I basically shout, holding out his mostly dry shirt and boxers. "Your pants aren't dry, but for the love of all that's holy, please put these on."

Brock bites down on his bottom lip and draws his head back ever so slightly, assessing me. "Why? Gettin' a little hot and bothered, Abby Jane?"

I shoot him what I hope is a fierce scowl. "By you? Never. Just tired of looking at your lackluster"—I swirl my hand in the general direction of his magnificent body—"attributes."

Brock rises from the couch, stepping into my space. He grabs my wrist and runs it over his midsection, the muscles flexing under my touch. "Ain't nothing lackluster about me, babe." I yank my hand away as he steps back, a wide, knowing smile plastered across his stupidly handsome face. "Be a good girl and turn around so I can get dressed."

I hear rustling and then silence.

"Are…are you decent?"

"Why don't you face me and find out?"

"Um." Slowly, I do as he says. Praise all the angels in heaven, he's dressed. Well, as dressed as one can be, sans pants. "Wonderful. Let's hit the books." Brock smiles a placating smile at me but gets to work all the same.

Before I know it, an hour has passed, and our study guides are complete. "Think you're ready for the quiz next week?" I ask as I close my laptop.

"Yeah, I really do." He arches his back and stretches his arms over his head, a huge yawn passing his lips before he checks the time. "Damn, when did it get so late?"

"What time is it?" I feel around for my phone, but he beats me to it.

"Almost nine."

"Wow! Time flies…" I trail off, because really, what the fuck am I gonna say? *Time flies when you're ogling your former childhood friend.* Yeah, how about not.

Brock nods. "Guess I better head out." Just as he moves to re-pack his bookbag, a monstrous rumble of thunder rattles the walls of my apartment and the lights flicker off and then back on.

We both walk to my living room window, and I move the blinds so we can peer out. "Damn," I murmur, taking in swirling treetops and still-pounding rain. "I didn't realize it was that bad."

Shrugging his wide shoulders, Brock moves past me and heads for the laundry room. Like an eager puppy, I follow. Right as he opens the dryer, the lights die out. Only this time, they don't come back on. I fumble around in the dark, running my hand over the shelf above the washer and dryer until I feel the handle of my trusty flashlight. I grab it down and flick it on, the single beam illuminating the small room.

I lay my hand on Brock's shoulder, barely able to believe the question I'm about to ask. "Do…do you wanna just crash here tonight?"

CHAPTER NINE

BROCK

I tense at Abby Jane's question. I know me staying here probably isn't a good idea, but it's damn sure a better alternative than driving home in this weather.

"You sure?" I ask, turning to face her, causing her hand to fall away from my shoulder. I immediately miss the heat of her touch…like I said, this is a bad idea.

"Yeah. I'd feel awful if anything happened to you." She nibbles on her lip, looking every bit as vulnerable as she sounds.

"Why, Abs, are you tryin' to say you like me? You *really* like me?" She rolls her eyes but otherwise doesn't respond. "C'mon, you can admit it. They say it helps."

"It's not so much you that I like as much as having a clear conscience. So, you gonna stay or not?"

"Yeah, I'll stay. How're we gonna do this? Because while your couch was fine to study on, there's no way in hell my tall ass is sleeping on it."

"Got a bed in the guestroom." She shrugs a shoulder. "Will that work, your highness?"

"Yeah, firecracker, that'll work just fine." The

nickname slips out, and Abby Jane rears back ever so slightly.

"Firecracker?" she asks, her dark eyes drinking me in as she awaits my answer.

"Yeah. It suits you. You burn hot, and you're a little unpredictable."

She smirks and crosses her arms over her chest, pushing her tits up a little higher. "I knew you thought I was hot."

"Not what I said," I counter, though she's right. I do. "But you tell yourself whatever you need to hear."

"Whatever. I'm gonna go get ready for bed. Guestroom's all yours. Bathroom is across the hall. G'night." She passes me her flashlight and sets off down the dark hall.

"Sleep tight, Abby Jane," I holler after her retreating form, all the while wondering what exactly she sleeps in.

I open the door to the guestroom and instantly notice there's not a bed in sight. No. There's a damn futon. *Dammit, Abs.* Guess it's still better than driving home during a fucking monsoon.

After stripping off my shirt, I settle down onto the futon. I toss and turn for what feels like a small eternity, but try as I might, I can't get comfortable. The mattress is thinner than a damn beach towel, and no matter how I lay, the metal bar presses into my back. There's no way in hell this is gonna work.

Guess it's time to find out just what Abby Jane

sleeps in.

Quietly, I nudge open her partially closed door. Through the darkness, I can see Abby Jane's sleeping form taking up most of the king-sized bed. Figures she'd be a bed hog...then again, she was as a kid, too. Some things really never do change.

I approach the left side, since there's a bit more room, and slide under the covers. Abby Jane immediately wakes up, bolting to an upright position with a yell. "What the fuck are you doing in here?"

"Ain't no way I'm sleeping on that piece of shit futon." She huffs, and I smile big and wide. "Now, move over and share like the nice girl I know you are deep, *deep* down."

Abby Jane angrily shifts over, farther away from me, and her bare leg brushes mine. "I swear to God, you're a menace."

"That may be true, but I'm gonna be a well-rested menace. Go to sleep."

We fall silent, me lying on my back and Abby Jane with her back to me. It's not long before her soft snores fill the room, lulling me to sleep as well.

I wake before the sun, and sweet merciful baby Jesus, my rock-hard dick is cradled between Abby Jane's ass cheeks like it's begging for entrance. Legit, the only thing keeping me out—you know, other than her lack of consent—is the two thin layers of our underwear.

Yeah, that's right. Abby Jane sleeps in her panties. I know this because my hand seems to have found its way to her thigh in our sleep, with my thumb almost brushing against the promised land, and judging by all the smooth skin under my touch, sleep shorts aren't an option. Unless they're the size of a fucking postage stamp.

Still sleeping, she pushes her ass back farther, eliciting a deep groan from me. "Abs, you gotta stop."

She lets out a soft moan followed by a mumbled, "Don't wanna." And as much as I want her to mean that, I know it's the sleep talking.

"Abby Jane." Her name comes out sounding more like a prayer, but my plea falls on deaf ears as she rolls her hips, causing a throb in my groin.

She rolls to face me, and I brace myself, prepared for her to light into me. Instead, she shocks the shit out of me and presses an open-mouthed kiss to my clavicle, her teeth grazing it lightly as she moves toward my neck.

Panting like a fucking fifteen-year-old getting his first bit of action, I ask, "Wh-what are you doing?"

"Shh," she hisses against my skin. "Don't ruin this with your big mouth."

Her words spur me into action, and I haul her up from my side so that she's straddling me, diving for her mouth as soon as her thighs clamp around mine. Our kiss is like Paul Walker in *The Fast and the Furious*—zero to one hundred in less than sixty seconds.

REBEL HEART

Abby rocks against me, and we both moan. I don't know what alternate reality I woke up into this morning, but Jesus, I really, really like it.

Just like I love the way her weight feels on top of me…the heat of her lithe body pressing down on mine. I love her taste and the softness of her lips and skin.

Desperate to see all of her, she pulls her shirt over her head, baring her beautiful, perky, *pierced* breasts to me. Holy hell. Never in a million years would I have ever thought barbells through a chick's nipples were hot but on Abby Jane? It's downright sexy, and I can't wait one more second to have them in my mouth.

Unfortunately for me, that's when she comes to her senses and pushes me away before flying off of me in search of her shirt. She pulls it back over her head, muttering and mumbling up a storm as she stalks into her closet, only to return fully covered, in a pair of sleep pants.

Quizzically, I lift a brow at her, but she pays me no mind, stomping out of her room and down the hall. Jesus Christ—that fine line between love and hate? Yeah…we just obliterated it—only, I'm pretty sure she still hates me.

Trepidatiously, I follow behind her, making a pitstop in the spare bedroom to grab my shirt and bag. From behind me, Abby calls out, "Here." She tosses my jeans at my feet and rushes back out of the room.

I shimmy into my jeans and make my way out to the living room, but she's nowhere in sight. A quick glance down the hall shows her bedroom door is now shut. If I had to guess, I'd say she's hiding out in there—hiding from me.

My pride won't let me stay where I'm not wanted, so without a word, I slip my shoes on and let myself out.

CHAPTER TEN

AJ

Oh, Jesus, what have I done? What the fuck was I thinking? I pace back and forth in front of my bed—the same bed where I almost let Brock into my panties. Brock... the same boy who went from being my best friend to ignoring my existence altogether in middle school. Like a scratched CD, the same thoughts loop through my mind. I fling myself down onto the mattress, and instantly, I'm assaulted with the memory of his five o'clock shadow brushing against my cheek, reminding me that he's no longer that boy, but a man. "Seriously, what the fuck?"

How could something so wrong feel so right? How could Brock Larson, of all people, make me feel like that? Like I was weightless and heavy all at once. Like I was desired and sexy and coveted. *How?* He contradicts almost everything I stand for.

While I shun my silver-spoon upbringing, he wears his like a badge. I refuse to comply with my parents' expectations, and he falls in line like a good little soldier. I yearn for passionate, crazy, uncontrollable love that burns like a wildfire, whereas he probably wants a society wife, with her pearls in place and hair perfectly coifed, to meet him at the door every night, scotch in hand and dinner on the table.

No matter how much he turns me on, we'd never work. And while I'm no prude, I know better than to shit where I eat, so to speak. Hooking up with Brock wouldn't lead to anything good. No way, no how. Especially if word ever got around to our parents. His dad would probably forbid it, and mine would either expect me to fall in line and conform to their insane standards or—and this is more likely—they would be worried about me tainting their sweet and perfect Brock with my wickedness. You know, because wild hair and tattoos equal wickedness.

Slowly, I move from mild irritation to outright anger. Fuck him for starting something with me after the way he walked out of my life all those years ago. Fuck him for crawling into my bed, damn near naked, like the biggest temptation I've ever seen. Fuck him for making me feel desired, wanted, and worthy, all with his lips pressed to mine.

The feeling of dampness on my cheeks blankets the rage simmering in my veins. *Am I seriously crying over this? Over him?* No. Nope. No way. Never.

Unwilling to waste my tears on an almost hook-up with a pretty-boy who probably has a different airhead warming his sheets every weekend, I snatch my phone off the charging dock and text Stacia a *911* message,

REBEL HEART

knowing she'll have to respond no matter what. That's our code, and Lord knows, she's sent me enough of them over the years.

Me: 911!!

Stacia: REALLY? WHY? WHAT?

Me: Late breakfast before my class?

Stacia: Benny's?

Me: Duh.

Stacia: I'll park at yours and we can walk together.

Fifteen minutes later, I'm dressed in my most favorite cut-off denim shorts and a cotton crop top that reads '*But first coffee*' across it, waiting in the lobby for Stacia. Luckily, I've only been waiting a few minutes when she strolls through the door. "Ready?"

"Yup. Let's go."

We exit the lobby, and Stacia pounces before I can even take a step from under the awning. "Why the 911 text?"

"I…ugh. It's so stupid."

Stacia turns to face me, her eyes glowing with intrigue. "Seriously, talk to me. I can't help if I don't know."

I pinch my eyes shut and suck in a deep breath of fresh air and slowly blow it out before pulling her behind me and onto the sidewalk. Once we're on our way toward Benny's, I launch into why I summoned her, not skipping over a single detail. "So, as you can see, I messed up."

"Oh AJ," Stacia murmurs, her voice full of sympathy. "Don't get mad at me, okay?" She pauses and I nod. "Did you really mess up though?"

I scrunch my nose at her question. "What do you mean? Of course I did. I almost slept with Brock!"

"No, I heard you. Now, hear me. He's not some rando dude from the bar. He's not married or in a relationship. Sure, y'all have a tumultuous history, but maybe it's not such a bad thing?"

Ugggh. I massage my temples, contemplating ways to make her see things my way. "How? How can you say that? He's...him, and I'm...me. We're so totally opposite, and we can hardly stand each other for more than five minutes at a time!"

"C'mon now, girl. You know as well as I do that opposites attract. And anyone with eyes can see how fine he is. Not to mention, you're always saying you want that crazy kind of love…"

Her words leave me a little stunned and I almost walk into a bench. "Right. But I don't love Brock. I borderline hate him."

Stacia tsks me. "There's a fine line between love and hate, AJ."

"That may be so, but I can guarantee you, there's no love between us. Lust? Sure. Love? Never. Not ever in a million years."

Smirking, she sing-songs, "Never say never, bitch!"

"Enough about this. I need a change of subject." I quicken my pace to an almost speed-walk. "And some bacon in my belly, pronto!"

Benny's—our favorite little diner—is in sight when the sound of loud exhaust pipes and a growling engine fill the air. Instinctually, I glance toward the racket, my eyes landing on none other than Brock's big beast of a truck. After last night and this morning, I can unequivocally say he's not compensating for anything.

He slows as he approaches us, coming to a stop in the middle of the damn road. "Great. Just great," I mutter as he rolls his window down.

"Are you following me?" I snap at him, ready and willing to settle for something else to eat if it means avoiding him.

He pins me with a hard stare, looking a little rumpled, but no worse for wear. "Nah, Abby Jane. Believe it or not, my world doesn't revolve around you. I've actually got a life and responsibilities, not that you know anything about that."

"Are you implying I don't have responsibilities of my own?"

He smirks. "If the shoe fits…"

Ready to tear him a new asshole, I step toward his truck, but his next words stop me short. "Good luck on the quiz today, Abby Jane. Just so you know…I aced it."

I stand there, gaping at him as he punches the gas, leaving me fuming on the side of the road. *I swear to God, if thoughts of his stupid, smug self distract me from acing this quiz...* At least he's not in Professor Doss's Friday class with me.

Stacia's cheeks split into a knowing grin. "Well, y'all burn hot, that's for sure."

Shaking off the funk he's left me in, I paste a fake-ass smile across my face. "New rule: we don't talk about him or anything involving him." I link our arms and drag her toward the diner that's just across the street. "He's nothing but a pompous, self-righteous ass."

I can tell my bestie has more to say on the subject, but thankfully she holds her tongue. I make it through class, and I'm eighty-seven percent positive I aced my quiz. Lord knows, I better have, or I'll ream Brock's stuck-up, entitled ass clear into next week.

The rest of my Friday is pretty uneventful—you know, aside from me stressing out over that small thirteen percent uncertainty over my grade. Not in the mood to be social, I decide to stay home and enjoy a beer in the comfort of my jammies while curled up on the couch watching *The Mindy Project*.

I blink myself awake around noon, only to find myself still agitated. Desperate to shake off this funk, I invite Stacia over and knowing me the way she does, she shows up with a paper bag full of tacos, salsa, and cheese dip in one hand and a bag of fries in the other.

I immediately snatch both bags from her and set to work. Unceremoniously I dump the fries onto a large plate before deconstructing the tacos and sprinkling the meat over the fries. I then top it off with cheese dip and salsa, plus a dollop of sour cream from my fridge. *Gah. If you haven't gorged on taco fries, have you even really lived?*

Once we're settled on the couch, Stacia wastes no time starting in on me. "So, about Brock…" However, I've placed him in my mental no-fly zone. So, I quickly shut her down and redirect our conversation.

"Nope! More important things to discuss…like what we're bingeing today."

Stacia rolls her eyes at me but doesn't press the issue. "*New Girl?*" she asks.

"Always," I confirm, because good God, I love me some Schmidt.

We watch enough episodes that we have to confirm we're still watching four times. On the fifth, we decide to break for dinner—Cup-O-Noodles for the win. We sit in silence, savoring our cheap-ass, quintessential college meal, twirling the noodles and slurping them off of our forks.

"Fuck," Stacia mumbles around a mouthful. "Why's this shit so good?"

With my mouth just as full as hers, I reply. "Don't know, don't care." I lift the Styrofoam cup to my lips and drink some of the spicy chicken broth and wipe my mouth on the back of my hand. "Oh, hey! Wanna stay the night?"

"Duh, bitch. Duh."

After disposing of our dinner trash, we pop two bags of popcorn and continue our binge-fest until we both fall asleep on the couch. I wake up around three in the morning with a crick in my neck from laying my head against the armrest. Stacia's legs are tangled together with mine, but she was smart enough to lay her head on a pillow.

Carefully, I slide off of the couch, and after a long stretch, I grab a quilt from the laundry room and drape it over her before heading back to sleep in my own bed.

Stacia, early riser that she is, wakes me up around nine, bouncing on my bed on all fours. "Wake up!"—Bounce—"Wake up!"—Bounce, again and again. I try to ignore her, hoping she'll give up and go away, but no such luck. "Wake your ass up, or I'm gonna lick you!"

"Ugh. Fine. I'm up. Keep your morning-breathed tongue to yourself."

"Yay!" she hoots.

I wipe the sleep from my eyes, expecting to see her still in the clothes she fell asleep in. But she's not. Nope. That bitch is freshly showered and dressed in clothes from my damn closet. I quirk a brow at her, and she shrugs.

"Get showered and dressed, for today, we brunch!"

I cringe at her loud tone but shuffle to the bathroom all the same.

We settle on Bay Harbor—a cute little bistro down by the water. Over caramel-soaked French toast and mimosas, she tries once again to breach the Brock subject, but like before, I change the subject. I know she can see right through me, but I also know that she knows I'll talk when I'm good and ready and not a second before.

After brunch, we hit the mall. A new pair of Nike SB sneakers and a few tops later, Stacia jets off to meet her parents for an early dinner, and I head back to my apartment. Thoughts of Brock threaten to creep in, and I'm almost tempted to text him, which means I need a diversion.

Even though I showered this morning, I run myself a bubble bath, determined to soak the thoughts of him away. While the tub fills, I lean my head over the side and wet my hair down so I can apply a liberal dose of my pink color-depositing conditioner. I comb it through and pile my hair on the top of my head, securing it with an alligator clip.

Stepping into the tub, I sink down into the hot, steamy water and grab my Kindle from the little table I set up next to the bath. I tap open my latest read—a sexy rom-com about a sex therapist who has a thing for young, William Levi lookalikes but finds herself falling for a slightly older single dad. I'm so lost in the pages of my latest book, I don't even realize my conditioner's been sitting for half an hour and my water's cold.

After I drain the tub, I hop in the shower to rinse my hair and decide while I'm there that I may as well go all out on a full pampering session; I exfoliate, shave, and do a face mask. Hell, by the time I'm finished, my skin is tinged pink from the hot water, and I'm squeaky clean.

With my skin still damp, I massage my Love Spell lotion in all over. The sweet fragrance almost makes me think of Brock and his shower activities, but I stay strong and toss my hair up in a towel, resolute in my intention to think of *anything* other than him.

I throw on a pair of panties and a tank top and decide to tidy up my apartment. Once every surface is gleaming, I chow down on a bowl of cereal and crack open my laptop to work on getting ahead in a few of my classes—really all of them, except British Lit, because that class makes me think of you-know-who.

By the time bedtime rolls around, I'm proud as fuck of myself, because I haven't thought of him not even once. Not really, I mean, until now. But this totally doesn't count because I'm only thinking of him to congratulate myself for not thinking of him.

CHAPTER ELEVEN

BROCK

Abby Jane and I seem to be stuck in a holding pattern, and to say I'm over it would be a gross understatement. The girl runs more and hot and cold than that damn Katy Perry song. Tonight, at tutoring, I'm putting an end to this stupid-ass game once and for all.

As if my stress levels aren't high enough between my tumultuous relationship with Abby Jane, classes three days a week, tutoring two, volunteering one, golfing all fucking seven—and that doesn't even count actual tournaments—Amanda blew up my phone all damn weekend. I managed to dodge her, but something tells me my luck is running out where she's concerned.

Just gonna go ahead and add that to the list of shit I don't want to think about. Other items on said list include my douchebag father and his expectations, and how the hell I'm going to continue at this pace. While I do my best not to show it, I need a break.

I'm heading out of the weight room when Coach Murphy yells my name.

I pivot in place to face him. "Yes, sir?"

"I trust you're on track with that class of yours?"

"Yes, sir. Tutoring is helping. We had a quiz this past Wednesday—I killed it."

"Good. Keep it up," he says, turning and walking away, effectively dismissing me.

Like every Tuesday, I rush home and change into a pair of khakis and a polo before grabbing lunch and heading to the course. Unlike every Tuesday, today my phone pings with an incoming text from my father asking me to call him. *Asking. Like I actually have an option.* Fucking asshole.

Grudgingly, I hit the call icon next to his name and the sound of ringing filters out through my truck's speakers. "Took you long enough," he snaps in lieu of a normal, civil greeting.

"Less than two minutes, Dad. I literally just got your text."

"I sent it five minutes ago, Brock." He sounds so put out to have waited on me for three minutes.

"I don't know what to tell you, Dad. But I have the time stamp on my phone saying when it came through."

"Enough with this childishness. I need you to stop by the house when you finish at the links."

I hold in my sigh, even though it almost kills me. "Yes, sir, but I can't stay long. I have—"

He cuts me off. "Great. See you then."

"Sure thing. Wasn't like I was talking," I mutter, even though he can't hear me. God, he's such a pompous, self-obsessed jackass.

REBEL HEART

My earlier phone call with dear old dad has me off my game. I'm shooting over par and landing my ball in every goddamn hazard on the course. After the first eighteen holes, I've had it, and decide to ride the cart as the guys work their way through the next eighteen.

Normally we would give a guy shit for sitting out, but I think they can tell I'm in no mood to be fucked with, because they don't say a word, acting like it's the most normal thing on earth.

I'm so busy obsessing over why I've been summoned to my childhood home, I don't even realize we've made it back to the clubhouse. But the second I do, I haul ass from the cart to my truck, not even bothering to tell anyone goodbye.

On the drive from the course, dread sits heavy in my gut. The feeling only intensifies when the house comes into view. It looms on the horizon, big and imposing, a stucco mansion with oversized columns and a grand staircase. I roll to a stop at the iron security gate, waiting for it to pick up on my sensor so I can pass.

I creep up the steps, slightly nauseated, and knock on the front door. Promptly Marta—our house manager—swings it open and greets me. "Mr. Larson. Your parents are waiting for you in the family room."

I almost snort at her use of the term family room, because *fuck*, you could hardly call us a family. All the same, I tip my chin to her and set off to meet whatever bullshit Dad has thought up for me now.

"Brock!" my father booms when I enter the room. "Just like you to keep us waiting. Sit. Let's talk." I clench my fists and jaw to keep from rolling my eyes as I walk over to the couch.

"Where's Mom?" I ask, but I already know the answer.

"She's resting," he says brusquely, leaving it at that. Except I know *resting* is code for avoiding his arrogant ass.

He stalks over to the beverage cart and pours two fingers of whiskey into his glass before raising the glass, looking at it from this way and that before sniffing. He's so fucking pretentious, going through this entire charade, like his whiskey isn't the best of the best—like he has to inspect it every damn time. Surprise, surprise, he finds it to his liking. He makes a big show of adding a few drops of water to it, but not once does he offer me a drink.

He positions himself in the wingback chair directly across from where I'm seated and rests his left ankle on his right knee, his posture ramrod straight. He keeps his eyes locked on mine as he takes a drink.

Finally, I get fed up with him and snap. "Want to tell me why I'm here any time soon? I have somewhere I need to be."

"You'll leave when I dismiss you, son, and not a second before." He speaks with conviction, like what he's saying is normal and acceptable.

REBEL HEART

"Dad. Why am I here? To talk about my grades? Golf? What?"

He shakes his head as if I'm amusing him. "Brock. I already know your grades and how you're performing on the field. I have eyes and ears everywhere."

I draw my head back and look at him. *Eyes and ears everywhere...*what kind of crazy bullshit is he spouting now.

"I've heard you've been...spending time with Charles and Elenore's wayward daughter."

I huff out a laugh. Funny how things change. From birth, our parents arranged play dates for us; yet now, in the eyes of Everett Larson, Abby Jane no longer measures up. Our families consider her a blemish on their reputations. How fucking archaic is that? A woman having her own style, thoughts, and opinions being frowned upon in this day and age—but, in the upper-crust-old-money-our-shit-doesn't-stink-posse, it's just a way of life.

"Yeah, she's my tutor," I say slowly.

Dad grits his teeth, but nods. "One: it's 'yes sir' not 'yeah.' And two: in order to make sure you're making wise decisions, I've arranged for Amanda to join us for dinner toni—"

I leap from the where I'm seated on the couch. "I *just* said I had somewhere I needed to be! Do you ever listen?"

With sharp precision, he reaches out and strikes his open palm across my cheek. "Do. Not. Interrupt. Me!"

he yells, spittle flying from his lips.

I stagger back from him, shocked that he physically laid his hands on me. All my life, he's wielded words as his weapon of choice, but I guess there truly is a first time for everything. Or, hell, maybe this was a long time coming. As long as he's hitting me and not Mom. My cheek stings, but I refuse to show any outward appearance of pain.

"Now, as I was saying, I've invited Amanda to join us for dinner tonight. You *will* join us. You *will* have a good attitude. And you *will* enjoy her company. She's charming and has a remarkable pedigree."

Charming is the last word I'd ever use to describe Amanda Burkett. Instead, words like psycho and stage five clinger come to mind. I twist my neck from side-to-side, finding satisfaction in the cracking sound it makes as some of the tension leaves my body. "Great. Let me just step out and make a quick phone call."

Without waiting for a reply, I stalk through the house and out the front door. Only, instead of crossing the threshold to freedom, I come face-to-face with the devil herself.

"Brocky!" Amanda shrieks in that whiny voice she uses when she wants to sound seductive. I cringe at the shrill timbre and take her in. She's dressed in a pressed white blouse with a modest, square neckline that's tucked into the wide band of her pastel patterned skirt that flares around her slim calves. Her feet are clad in some ropey wedge sandals, and pearls adorn her ears and neck. She looks like Susie-freaking-Homemaker. A perfect, demure debutante—a wolf in sheep's clothing.

She links her arm with mine and drags me back into the house, walking through it like she owns it. Then again, I'd bet my left nut she's actively planning on owning it one day—as my wife. *Fat fucking chance.*

"Amanda," I say her name sternly, halting our progress. "I was headed outside to make a call."

She parts her pale pink slicked lips to reply, but my father speaks over her. "My darling girl." He leans down and air kisses her cheek. "So glad you could join us this evening. Your company is always an honor."

She giggles and blushes. "Oh, Mr. Larson, you sure have a way with words." *Yeah, the fuck he does—his smooth words keep everyone eating out of the palm of his hand. And apparently when his words fail, his palm fucking seals the deal.*

"Are you kids ready to eat? The chef has prepared a proper feast."

"Actually, I still need to make that phone call," I inform him, deeply regretting leaving my phone in the car thinking I'd only be here briefly.

"Nonsense. Any phone call you need to make can wait until after dinner. Wouldn't want to eat cold food."

"Your dad's right, Brocky." She clasps my hand in hers and all but drags me behind her to the dining room. *Ugh. Neither of them is right. I'm already on thin ice with Abby Jane and ditching her tonight will probably send me through the ice and into the freezing water.*

The only upside to this shit-tastic evening is seeing my mom seated on the far side of the table, just to the right of where my father will sit at the head of the table. "Brock," she coos, sounding frustrated and happy all at once.

I rush to her side and wrap my arms around her. "How are you?" I whisper in her ear, but she doesn't reply. Instead, she pulls back ever so slightly and studies my face before echoing the question back to me. "I'm okay, Mom. Promise."

Ever the diplomat—even if sometimes, thanks to my dad, she's more like a doormat—she gently addresses Amanda next. "Hello, so nice to see you. I trust your parents are well?"

Amanda takes the seat next to my mother and launches into a no-details-spared update of her parents. I claim the chair to the left of my father and across from the women, content to let Amanda ramble if it means I don't have to engage.

Fortunately, Amanda and my father monopolize the conversation until our food is served and once our plates are placed before us, their chatter tapers off. Our meal consists of baked Cornish hen in a lemon butter and thyme sauce, served alongside roasted fingerling potatoes and crisp asparagus, but I can barely taste it because I'm so damn worried about things with Abby Jane. She's probably going to cut off my testicles and force feed them to me.

Unfortunately, the meal's over too soon and

conversation picks right back up. "Amanda," my father says. "Tell me, do you have any plans this weekend?"

She bats her lashes at him and my food churns in my gut. "No sir, I don't."

"Wonderful, because before you arrived, Brock was telling me how much he'd love to take you for dinner." *The fuck I was!* The words are on the tip of my tongue, tasting like bile, but I swallow them down.

Amanda swings her bright blue gaze over to me. "You were?" She sounds breathless. I swear, if I could kill my dad right now, I would. I mean, not literally, but, you know.

I once again crack my neck, followed by my knuckles. Anything to buy myself some time to regain my inner composure. "Absolutely," I say through gritted teeth—*so much for composure*—even though I have no plans on following through. I'll figure out some way to cancel later.

Hours after arriving, dinner is finally over, and I'm free to leave. Finally free to call Abs and beg her forgiveness. I walk Amanda to her car with the intention of canceling our plans, but my words seem to go in one ear and out the other. "Amanda, did you hear me?"

She sighs softly and places her hand on my chest. "I heard you, Brock. You're too busy for dinner this weekend. But that's plumb silly. We both have to eat. To save you some time, I'll drive myself and meet you. Saturday, seven-thirty, at Thyme." She rises to her tippy toes and presses her lips to my cheek before getting into her sparkly new Benz and driving away, not giving me another chance to rebuff her.

Why can't this girl take no for an answer? And better yet, why is she so fucking obsessed with me?

CHAPTER TWELVE

AJ

Even though I managed to get through most of the weekend and Monday without thinking about Brock, today he has been the only thing occupying my mind. My thoughts today have ranged from regret over how we left things to lust because he's just so…*something*…so sexy and masculine and sure of himself. I've thought of telling him we should put our shit aside and just get through our sessions just as much as I've considered telling him we should casually hook up all the while, just to scratch the itch.

But now that I've been sitting here in the library for over half an hour working alone while waiting for him to show—all thoughts of forgiveness and reconciliation are long fucking gone. I've texted him no less than five times, my messages ranging from a simple "Where are you?" to "Are you okay?" to "I swear to God, you better have a good reason for not showing." Yet all of them have gone unanswered. For a split second I worry that maybe he was in an accident or something, but I shake it off. I'm sure he's fucking fine and just being a dick.

Apparently, my time is worthless to him, and I should've trusted my gut instincts. He's nothing more than a spoiled little prick who thinks the world revolves around him. All he had to do was text me and let me know he couldn't make it.

Or call. An email. A goddamn carrier pigeon. Anything. But nope. Not a word. He hasn't bothered to do any of the following. Guess I know what I'm worth to him now. And as much as I hate to admit it…it kind of hurts.

I decide to call him before I pack up and leave. Straight to voicemail. *Shocking.* After the beep, I leave him a message telling him exactly how I feel. I tell him he's a self-obsessed jackass, and that our tutoring sessions are as good as done and not to bother calling back.

The satisfaction of chewing out his voicemail only lasts about five minutes before the melancholy sets in, because if I'm being honest, Brock was starting to grow on me—like mold, but still. And truthfully, I enjoyed our bickering. I loved seeing glimpses of the boy I called my best friend for so long. But I made it the past eight years without him by my side, and I damn sure know I'll make it now, too.

Angrily, I shove my shit into my bag and stomp out to my car. I sling my bag onto the passenger floorboard and sink down into the driver's seat, relishing the way the worn leather feels against my skin. I crank the ignition and drive the few blocks back to my apartment, fighting tears the whole way.

Finally, once I'm safely inside, I let them fall. Fuck him. Fuck him for throwing me away all over again and fuck me for caring so much.

That last thought is sobering, and I steel my resolve. He doesn't care about me? Then I don't care about him. As childish and petty as that sounds, I really don't care, because from here on out, I'm only looking out for *numero uno*—me.

Buzz. Buuuuuzzzzz. Buzz.

The sound of my phone vibrating against my nightstand wakes me out of a dead sleep. I peel one eyelid open and check the time, shocked to see it's only seven. *Jesus!* I don't even remember falling asleep; I guess I passed out when I snuggled up in bed to read.

Even though it's a perfectly acceptable time to text, I'm pissed that it woke me up. Obviously my body needed the sleep. I stretch and stand from the bed—whoever's blowing up my phone can wait—and pad into the kitchen to grab a glass of water and a Nutella Uncrustable.

I step back into my bedroom and set my sandwich and glass on the nightstand next to my still buzzing phone. Agitated, I snatch it up and unlock it with my index finger. I have four missed calls from Brock, along with a slew of texts. *Too bad it's too late, Jockstrap.*

I drag down my notifications bar and read the

preview of his last message. And while I can't see more than *Abby Jane, please let me expla...*I already know it's probably nothing more than him trying to pass off some half-assed apology. Yeah, not gonna happen. I tap *Reply* and quickly inform him that he can fuck right off before deleting our text thread and setting my phone to the Do Not Disturb setting.

The guilt for deleting our thread without ever reading his texts sets in almost immediately. God, I hate being so wishy-washy. One of the things I've always prided myself on was knowing what I wanted or felt and sticking to my guns about it. But since Brock's reentered my life, I've turned into a second-guesser, and it's got to stop.

I'm seated at the kitchen bar studying Wednesday night when my phone rings. It's Brock. Exasperated with his incessant calling, I answer. "What?"

"How nice of you to finally answer."

"What? You don't like being kept waiting? Huh, imagine that."

"Jesus. I'm trying to apologize. Hell, I've *been* trying to apologize." He sounds as annoyed as I feel.

I pause for dramatic effect. "I'm waiting, Jockstrap."

"Listen, I'm sorry for standing you up. Family shit came up, and I didn't have my phone on me. Truly, Abs, I'm sorry."

I can hear sincerity in his voice, and I believe him

that something came up, but I'm still butthurt. "Great. Thanks for letting me know. Have a nice life."

"So, I'll see you tomorrow?"

"No," I say, drawing out the word. "Nope."

Indignant, he asks, "What do you mean no?"

Why do people have such a hard time with the word no? "I mean I'm not tutoring you anymore. Let's be honest, you don't even need it, and we can't seem to be civil for more than seven minutes at a time."

"That's not gonna work for me, Abby Jane. Plus, I happen to remember something about tutoring me for a letter of recommendation? Geez, I'd sure hate it if you didn't get that letter…." He pauses, letting his words sink in.

He wouldn't…

"See you tomorrow or else, Abs. Your choice," he says before ending the call. *That rat bastard…he would!*

CHAPTER THIRTEEN

BROCK

I get to the library fifteen minutes before our usual time and park myself on the top step. I'm not giving Abby Jane the chance to back out of this. Then again, she could always stand me up, but I've just gotta hope she wants the recommendation letter badly enough to show.

Guess I didn't need to worry after all, because at five o'clock on the dot, Abby Jane whips her beast of a car into a spot across the street. I stand as she approaches, ready to greet her, but she brushes right past me and into the library. Much to my shock, she takes us back to a small, private table. *Interesting development.* We both take our time getting situated, but we're only delaying the inevitable. This conversation we're about to have has been a long time coming.

I'm the first to break the uneasy silence. "Abs, let's talk…please?"

She huffs and rolls her eyes. "Fine. Talk."

Sexy, difficult woman. "Look, you know my dad's an ass. He forced me to stay for dinner, and I didn't have my phone on me. I should have tried harder to reach out to you. I'm sorry, okay? Please forgive me."

Her rigid posture slowly relaxes, and internally I pump my fist in victory. She's gonna forgive me. She blows out a long breath and gives me a small smile. "Fine. But this is strike two, Jockstrap. Three and you're out."

I bark out a laugh. "Abs. You know there aren't strikes in golf, right?" She bites her lip and shrugs. *Jesus. This girl.* Now that I know we're not going anywhere, I dig my phone and keys from my pockets and lay them on the table.

"You ready?" she asks, opening her book, alerting me to the fact that in my haste to beat her here, I must have left mine in my truck.

"Shit. Lemme run out and grab my book; I left it…"

She cuts me off. "Sure, Brock. But please hurry. We have a lot of shit to do before finals."

I push back my chair, smirking at how quickly she can switch gears—from pissed to playful to strictly business in two shakes of a lamb's tail. Quickly, I dash out and grab the book, which is right where I thought it was—on my dash. I rush to get back to Abby Jane, not wanting to run the risk of upsetting her and getting more sass from that smart mouth of hers.

Except, I guess I did take too long, because she doesn't look content, or even sassy. She looks outright pissed. I slow my approach, and hold my book out in front of me as if it can protect me from her ire. "You good, Abs?" I ask cautiously, not knowing what has her so upset.

She tips her chin my way in acknowledgment. "Mmm. Fine."

Aw, shit. She used the 'F' word. "Obviously you're not. Talk to me."

Abby Jane pins me with an ice glare. "You sure you wanna talk to me? Or would you rather talk to *Amanda*." She spits the words, anger and venom lacing her tone.

"Wh-what?" I ask, wondering how she even knows who Amanda is. Well, I mean, obviously she knows her; our parents run in the same circles. But that doesn't explain why she's bringing her up now.

"A-man-da." She breaks the name down by syllables, and it's then I notice my phone in her hand.

"You went through my phone?" I ask, my own anger rising to the surface.

"Right. Because that's the real issue." She lets out a humorless laugh. "And not the fact that you ditched me to eat dinner with fucking Amanda Burkett on Tuesday."

"That's not what happened, Abby Jane."

"Oh, it's not? So, she's lying?"

I scrub a hand over my face, trying to keep my cool. "Not what I said."

Abby Jane darts up from her chair, almost knocking it over in the process. "It can only be one or the other. She's lying, or you are."

I advance toward her, backing her slowly into a

stack. "No," I grit out. "No one is lying. I was coerced into dinner at my parents' house. They just happened to invite her to join us. A double fucking ambush and the last thing I need is lip from you about shit you do not understand."

Abby Jane opens her mouth to respond, but I tunnel my fingers into her silky pink hair and silence her with a hard press of my lips to hers. She immediately melts into me, moaning into my mouth, allowing me entrance. Our tongues tangle together in a fight for dominance until I nip at her bottom lips; she tastes like minty lip balm, coffee, and something uniquely Abby Jane.

With my fingers still in her hair, I give it a hard tug, tilting her face to deepen our kiss before trailing my hands down to her ass. I pull her hips into mine, and she doesn't hesitate—not even for a fucking second—to lift her legs and wrap them around me. In this position, my hardness is perfectly aligned with her heat, and oh, my *fucking* God, when she grinds into me, I just about lose my mind.

I can feel her heat through my goddamn khakis. "Are you wet for me, Abby Jane?" I ask against her lips before diving back into our kiss, not giving her time to answer. Because, really, we both know she is. Soaking, if I had to hazard a guess.

As voices filter in from the other side of the stack, our kiss slows until finally Abby Jane releases her legs from around my hips, and I let her slide down my body to the floor. The caveman in me roars when she lands on unsteady feet. She tilts her gaze up to mine, and I expect to see heat, but instead, I see vulnerability.

"Wh-what are we doing, Brock?"

"Fuck, Abs, I don't know." I pull on the ends of my hair. "I know a lot has happened between us over the years—" She tries to interrupt me, but I know I was a jerk back then, and it doesn't seem fair to move things forward with her without resolving our past. "I wish I had some grand reason behind the end of our friendship, but the truth is…I was a dick. Plain and simple.

"To be honest, I think I was half in love with you as a kid, but I also thought of you like a sister, which confused me. I didn't want to put the moves on you and risk our friendship, so instead when puberty hit and girls started showing interest, I thought with the wrong head—if you catch my drift—and ruined our friendship anyway. By high school, we weren't speaking at all, and since I'm already spilling my guts here…I've always regretted the way shit went down back then. I know it was shitty, and I know one apology won't make up for it." I run my hand along the side of her face before palming her cheek. "So, I guess all of that was a fucking longwinded way to say that while I don't know exactly what we're doing, I like it and I like you."

She nibbles on her lip and places both of her hands on my chest. "I like you too, even if you are a jackass."

"Yeah, well…you're kind of a bitch." She gasps, and I chuckle. "But it's all good because *bitchy* just so happens to look sexy as hell on you."

"So, what now?"

I release a long breath. "Well, as much as I'd like to say, 'Now, let's take this somewhere private and finish what we started,' I want to do things right with you." She beams up at me, and I know I've said exactly the right thing. "Plus, we need to study."

She draws her hands back from my chest before plopping them back down in a light, playful smack. "And…you ruined it."

"Let me take you to dinner tomorrow night, and I'll make it up to you."

Abby Jane's cheeks turn the prettiest shade of pink and damn if I don't want to pound on my chest in victory. "Okay, Brock. Pick me up at seven?"

"Will do. Now, let's get to work."

We both return to our seats and settle in, but every couple of minutes we exchange knowing glances. I'm guessing it's safe to say we're both excited for what's to come.

CHAPTER FOURTEEN

AJ

It's Friday evening, and I've spent the entire day anxious as fuck over my date tonight. So anxious that I called Stacia and asked her to come over and help me get ready. We're in the middle of twisting my hair up into this cute style I pinned the other week when Stacia finally asks what I can tell has been on the tip of her tongue since I called.

"Why are you so nervous, AJ? You've literally known Brock your entire life."

I must take too long to answer her, because she jabs one of my pink-painted bobby pins into my scalp. "Ow, bitch!" I swat her hands away and take over, carefully securing the pin so that my hair looks effortlessly messy. "And, I guess it's because this almost seems too good to be true."

I meet my bestie's eyes in the mirror and see she's frowning at me. "Um. What? No. Don't put yourself down like that."

"No. I misspoke. I don't think he is too good for me or anything. It's just…for so long he was my best friend in the entire world, and then one day…he just wasn't. I spent a long time hurt over that, and now, here I am, prepping for him to take me out. As a kid, I always thought we would be a 'thing' when we got to high school, but we fell out the second puberty hit. I can't help but wonder…*why now?*"

"Okay, okay. I can see that. But, worrying over it won't give you any answers, so turn around and let me do your eyeliner."

I do as she says, spinning and hoisting myself up onto my bathroom counter. I sit statue still while Stacia rims my eyes in my favorite liner—Perversion by Urban Decay. It is *life* and makes the best wings. When Stacia finishes, I keep my eyes closed for a few seconds to make sure the liquid is dry. When I do open my eyes, she stands back to make sure everything is even.

"Fucking perfection," she murmurs. "What lip color?"

"Blast Off," I tell her, referencing my favorite pink from Smashbox. It's a few shades brighter than my hair.

"Yes. So much fucking yes." With a practiced hand, she sets to work, dabbing a light coat of concealer across my lips, following it with clear lip liner before finally slicking on an even coating of my lipstick.

I hop down from the counter and turn to appraise my appearance. "Girl. Why aren't you in school for this?"

Stacia shrugs. "Business seemed like a safer choice."

Reaching out, I take her hands in mine. "Babycakes, not sharing your talent is a crime toward humanity."

Stacia rolls her eyes. "I wouldn't go that far."

"I would. You could easily be a platform artist or brand educator. And with a business degree on top of it, you could easily run your own empire." I pause, letting my words sink in. "At least think about it, okay?"

She rolls her lips inward and nods. "Okay. But enough about me. Brock will be here in thirty, and we need to get you dressed."

We stand side-by-side in my closet, rifling through potential outfits. "Ugh. This would be so much easier if I knew where we were going."

"AJ. Stop. Just wear something you feel sexy in."

Stacia's words spur me into action and I begin flinging hangers aside until I find exactly what I'm looking for. I wiggle my way into a pair of structured black leather shorts that stop mid-thigh, pairing them with a super soft gray tank and a black leather diagonal cut blazer. I layer several necklaces of varying lengths and slide my feet into a pair of pointy-toed, metal adorned black leather booties.

"Thoughts?"

"Um. I'll be shocked if y'all make it to wherever he plans on taking you. And if you don't wear it, I'll be taking it home with me."

I laugh and turn to assess my outfit one more time. The heels make my toned legs look a mile long, and the leather shorts hug my ass, accentuating it nicely. "Fuck yes. I'm gettin' some tonight!" I sing and Stacia holds her hand up for a high five.

"Yeah, you totally are." She lifts her wrist and checks the time on her smartwatch. "He'll be here in about ten minutes."

I walk back into my bathroom and lather myself with my Love Spell lotion and mist myself with the spray, knowing how much he loves this scent. Just as I step back into the bedroom, there's a knock on the front door. "Oh! He's early!"

"I'll go let him in. You finish up and head down when you're ready."

"Thanks, babe!" I holler after her already-retreating form.

I hear the front door open, and I strain my ears to hear their conversation, but it's no use. Quickly, I toss an extra pair of panties, my lipstick, and my phone charger into my bag. You know…just in case.

BROCK

I pull up to Abby Jane's damn near fifteen minutes early. Not wanting to look too eager, I kill time playing on my phone, checking the clock every two minutes. Finally, with only seven to spare, I decided I've waited long enough—especially when it already feels like I've waited a lifetime.

I opt to take the stairs up to her apartment, hoping

to rid myself of some of this nervous energy, but it's no use. Knowing that she's going to be on my arm tonight has me feeling like the luckiest motherfucker on earth.

When I reach her door, I take a deep, calming breath and knock. I'm expecting her to answer, so it throws me when her friend Stacia is who greets me instead. "Come on in. AJ'll be down in a sec."

"Tell her no rush, she can take all the secs…" I snap my mouth shut and shake my head at myself. "Fuck. Never mind."

Stacia laughs and quirks a brow at me. "Got sex on the brain, Mr. Larson?" When I don't reply, she keeps going. "Are you thinking about fucking Ms. Adams? About sticking your sausage into her love muffin?" Now we're both laughing. "Planning to play a rousing game of hide the salami? Or do you just want to eat her taco?"

It's that very minute Abby Jane steps into the room, and we immediately stifle our laughter. "Did someone say tacos?"

At that, Stacia and I lose it all over again. Stacia regains her composure first. "Well. Y'all have a lovely evening. Be safe—use condiments…I mean condoms."

Abby Jane gives us both a confused look. "What in the hell are you going on about?"

Stacia ushers us toward the door. "Nothing. Not a thing. Ignore me. Have fun! I'll lock up."

Abby shakes her head. "Whatever. You ready?"

It's then that I take in what she's wearing and my eyes about fall out of my head. I'm used to pearls, not leather, but as I rake my eyes over her smoking hot body, I swear to God never in my life have I been more thankful that Abby Jane marches to the beat of her own drum, because this outfit…*fuuuuuck.*

"Why are you staring at me?" she whispers.

"Because you look fucking incredible," I whisper back, my voice hoarse with need.

A throat clears, reminding me of two things. One, that we're not alone, and two, that we're loitering in Abby Jane's doorway.

I clasp Abs' hand in mine and tug her out into the hallway. "So, are we getting tacos?" Her voice is so hopeful, and I can't help but wonder what she'd think if she knew what we were really talking about.

"Uh. No. Not tonight. Maybe next time?"

"Already planning our next date, Jockstrap? Aren't you confident!"

"You think I'm letting you go after finally getting you? Hell no."

I ease my truck to a stop in the little back lot behind Vinny's and watch as Abby Jane's eyes light up. As kids, our parents always ordered takeout from here, and it's a Cottonwood staple through and through. "Really?" she asks, not bothering to hide her excitement.

"Yes, ma'am. Figured there's no better place for our first date."

"I bet you take all the girls here." She says the words

as a joke, but I still feel the need to set her straight.

"Nope. Never brought a girl here. In groups, sure. On a date? Never."

"R-really? Why?"

I shrug, trying to downplay my reason, because really, it's sort of dumb. "I don't know. This was always kind of *our* thing, Abs."

My answer must please her, because she presses her pretty pink lips to mine before turning and hopping down from my truck—which is no easy feat with how high it's lifted.

We meet at the back bumper and I loop my pinky finger around hers, guiding us around the building and toward the entrance. I pull the worn, red-and-glass paneled door open, allowing Abby Jane to enter first. The hostess stand has a sign up asking patrons to seat themselves, so with my hand pressed to the small of her back, we search out a table.

We settle on a rectangular two-seater near the door. After making sure Abby Jane's seated, I lower myself into the seat across from her. "You know, I've always loved the lighting in here," she says, referencing the cheese grater and wine bottle chandeliers. "As a kid, I was determined to have one like it in my kitchen."

"Hmm. I don't seem to recall any funky lighting in your apartment."

She laughs, and it warms me from the inside out. "Yeah, I grew out of it. But I still love to see it in here."

Right then, our server steps up to the table. "Hey,

y'all! Welcome to Vinny's. Our special pies are on the chalkboard. Y'all need a minute?"

I glance to Abby Jane and decide to take a chance. "Nope, we're ready to order. We'll both take draft root beers in frosted mugs, and we'll split a fourteen-inch pie, extra cheese, with pepperoni on all of it and black olives and green peppers on half."

"Got it. I'll grab your drinks and bring some bread." She pivots on her heel and heads back to the kitchen.

I turn to Abby Jane and find her gaping at me with wide eyes, looking slightly shell-shocked. "What? What's up?"

"You remembered?" Surprise paints her tone.

"Our order from back in the day? Fuck yeah, I remember. To be honest, there's not much about you I don't remember."

"Oh really?" she asks, her competitive side rising to the surface. "Okay then, when we were nine, what did I want to be when I grew up?"

I drum my fingers once on the tabletop. "Really? A quiz?"

She smirks. "I mean, if you don't know…"

"Well, to answer that question accurately, I'd need more info. Are you referring to at the end of third grade when you wanted to be an astronaut and begged your mom to send you to space camp? But she sent you to equestrian camp instead, and you changed your tune and decided you wanted to be a horse groomer, because you liked braiding their manes. Or maybe you mean the start of fourth grade when you wanted to be a veterinarian after helping treat one of the horses for a snake bite?"

When I'm finished, she sits there slack-jawed for a minute or two—long enough for our server to drop off our frosty mugs, two plates, and a platter of thick-sliced bread.

"Holy shit. You really do remember, huh?"

I pour a generous portion of olive oil onto my plate and dust it with some oregano and red pepper flakes. I tear off a bite of bread and run it through the oil before popping it into my mouth. After I swallow it, I take a long swig of my root beer. I know my silence is driving her a little bit crazy, so I decide to let her off the hook.

"Told ya. If it involves you, I remember."

We munch away on the bread until our server returns with our pizza and two fresh, frosty root beers. "Here y'all go. Lemme know if you need anything else." She carefully places the pan on the pizza stand, and I waste no time serving us both up two slices—pepperoni for me, added veggies for her.

Abby Jane lifts hers to her mouth and takes a bite, a string of gooey cheese connecting the slice to her lips. I reach out and wrap the strand around my thumb, severing it from the slice. With her eyes locked on mine, Abby Jane sets her slice down onto her plate and grabs my hand, sucking my thumb briefly into her mouth, ridding it of the cheese. I'm talking in and out in two seconds, but *Jesus*, I think I lived and died in those two seconds.

"So good," she moans as she digs back into her pizza. She's polished off an entire slice, and I haven't even started on mine. I've been too busy watching her eat, reveling in her little moans of satisfaction, obsessing over how it would feel to have other parts of me between those luscious lips of hers.

"Aren't you gonna eat?" she asks, nodding to my still-full plate.

Mentally, I shake off the haze I'm in. "Yeah, sorry. Got sidetracked."

We polish off the rest of our meal in a comfortable silence, and when our server comes by to ask if we'd like dessert, we decline, and I ask for the check. When she deposits it on the table, I can't hold back my laugh.

"What?" Abby Janes asks.

"Look." I spin the wooden board the bill is banded to toward her. "Read the band."

She scans it over, a huge smile breaking out across her face when she reads the words embossed into the band: *seven days without pizza makes one weak.* "Oh, my God. That is great. How have I never noticed that before?"

"I don't know, but I haven't either. It's fucking funny. I guess it's new?"

Just then our server reappears. "You mean the bands? Yeah. They're new. Just got them in this week. I'll have to tell Vinny y'all liked them. He was hesitant." She nods toward the board. "You ready for me to take that?

No rush or anything…"

I pull out my wallet and slide two twenties under the band. "We're good. Keep the change."

CHAPTER FIFTEEN

AJ

"Thank you for dinner," I say to Brock as he opens the passenger door of his truck for me. "It was delicious."

Brock backs me into the open door, causing the running boards to dig into my legs. He presses a soft kiss at the base of my neck—light and lingering, before working his way to my just below my ear. He gently traces my lobe with the tip of his tongue, sending shivers down my spine.

Unable to take any more of his torture, I grab his face and angle it toward mine, claiming his lips. He opens for me immediately, groaning into my mouth as he palms my ass and lifts me into the truck and pulls away.

We're both out of breath, and the wood he's sporting beneath his jeans is impressive—it's something I'd like to get intimately acquainted with. Brock catches me ogling his junk and reaches down and gives it a hard squeeze before adjusting himself. "Buckle up," he all but growls, and I fucking love knowing he's all worked up over me.

The drive from Vinny's back to my place is excruciating. I can't help but be curious about what's going to happen once we arrive. Is he going to come up? God, I hope so, and then he can go down…on me. The thought almost makes me moan out loud, and I shift in my seat, squeezing my thighs together.

"You okay over there?" Brock asks, smirking, not once taking his eyes off of the road.

"Mmhmm. Why?" I frown at how breathless my voice sounds.

"Just over there moanin' and wiggling in your seat."

Great. Guess I did moan out loud. "I'm just dandy. Don't you worry about me."

Brock guides his truck to a spot across the street from my apartment. "It's my job to worry about you. Now, c'mon, I'll walk you up."

I roll my eyes outwardly, but on the inside, that line melted me. "Okay, Casanova." Little does he know our night isn't ending here.

I press the call button for the elevator, and Brock stands directly behind me, so close the heat from his body covers mine. Ever so slowly, I push my ass into him, and now he's groaning. "You okay over there?" I ask, throwing his earlier words back at him.

He grips my hips with his strong hands and brings his lips to my ear and harshly whispers, "You're playin' with fire, Abby Jane."

The elevator doors open, and I step away from him and into the car; he follows and taps the button for the second floor. I step closer to him and palm his erection. "Good thing I like it hot," I whisper, and the words hang between us, mingling with our lust.

The doors open, and we file out and make it to my apartment. I slide my key into the lock and step over the threshold. "Aren't you gonna come in?"

"Maybe I shouldn't?" he asks, sounding torn.

I look up at him from beneath my lashes. "I *really* wish you would."

Brock scrubs a hand over his face. "Fuck, you really are a little firecracker." He steps in behind me and I close the door, sliding the lock into place.

Instantly he grips the back of my thighs and hoists me up. Our lips meet in a heated kiss; it's teeth and tongue and passion and longing all coming together at once. He lowers himself onto the couch so that I'm straddling him, and before I know it, I'm grinding down on him, and he's meeting me thrust for thrust.

Brock breaks our kiss and murmurs against my lips. "Fuck, Abs, you're so sexy. But I want to do things right with you."

I swivel my hips and his eyes roll back just a little. "No one gets to decide what's right but us."

"You sure?" he asks, ever the gentleman.

I lick my lips then shrug out of my blazer and tug my shirt over my head, leaving me bare on top since I skipped a bra. "One hundred and twenty percent. I want to finish what we started last time you were here." I bring my hands to my chest and tug on my nipple rings, moaning at the sensation. "I want to know how you feel inside me."

"Jesus Christ. That mouth of yours is trouble."

I shimmy out of his lap and sink to my knees on the floor, nestling myself between his spread legs. Brock watches me like a hawk as I flick open the button to his jeans before dragging the zipper down, freeing him from the confines of his pants. "Let me show you just how much trouble."

He lets out a guttural moan from deep in his throat when I hum against him. His hands tug on my hair as my fingers press into his thighs. I don't get to finish what I started before I'm being hauled up and laid back onto the floor. "As much as I love your kind of trouble, it's my turn."

Brock wastes no time stripping me: first my heels, then my shorts. My black lace panties give him pause, though. He stares at them like they're the eighth wonder of the world, rolling his lips as he does. "Damn. You are so sexy." His voice is sandpaper and grit, full of want.

With sure hands, he pulls the delicate lace from my body before pushing my legs farther apart. I shudder the moment his mouth lands where I need him the most, threading my fingers through his hair as he expertly works my body. "Tastes so good," he rumbles against my skin, and just like that, I fall apart, screaming his name.

Before I've even had a chance to recover, Brock moves from between my thighs to hovering over me. He seals his lips to mine in a searing kiss, nipping at my lip and then licking away the burn. He pulls back, and we're nose to nose. "Are you sure?"

"One hundred and twenty-five percent now," I reply with a sly grin.

He keeps his eyes on me, his eyes roaming over my exposed body, honing in on the colorful tattoos on my right side as he stands to kick off his shoes and finish the job I started of removing his pants.

I watch him just as intently as he pulls his wallet from his back pocket and snags a little foil packet. Sheathed and ready to go, Brock lowers himself back down to me and pushes inside, one hand supporting his weight while the other palms my cheek tenderly. He fits me like he was made for me, and he moves like he has a map to my pleasure points. He brings me to the edge again and again until we're both a sweating, panting mess of tangled limbs. But when I finally fall apart, he's right behind me, with a long, guttural, "Fuuuuck."

CHAPTER SIXTEEN

BROCK

Just when I think life can't get any better, Abby Jane shocks the shit out of me by asking if I want to stay the night. Obviously, I said yes. Hell. Yes.

So, here I am now, feeling like king of the fucking world, laying in my firecracker's bed with her my arm around her and her head on my chest. "You wanna watch a show?" she asks.

I drop a kiss to the top of her head and hold her a little closer before murmuring, "Sounds good."

She wiggles out of my hold to grab the remote, and I instantly miss the feel of her body pressed against mine. "Whatcha wanna watch?"

"It's up to you."

She turns to look at me, disbelief coloring her features. "Really?"

"Really. Do your worst, Abby Jane."

She clicks around, moving through Netflix like a wizard before settling on *Gossip Girl*. I smirk and pull her back into the position we were in. "You really think watching a little Serena and Blair is gonna upset me?"

"Oh, my God," she laughs. "You know their names?"

"Hell yeah. It's one of those guilty pleasure shows. West and I were watching a show one night and a rerun marathon came on after. Shit…we were six episodes in before we even realized what the fuck we were watching. Now, I've seen all of the seasons—at least twice."

Abby Jane runs her hand across my chest, lightly raking her nails as she goes. "You are something else, Brock. Not at all like I thought."

I hum deep in my throat. "Hush." My words are gruff. Tonight's been so damn perfect; I have no desire to ruin it by digging into the heavy shit. "We're getting to the good part of this episode."

Abby Jane passed out cold during the finale of the first season. I stayed up a little longer, despite my eyelids drooping—I wasn't ready for our night to end. I finally gave in and decided to call it quits at the start of the second season, just as Kristen Bell's voiceover told viewers, "Sex, lies, and scandal never take a vacation." I smirked at the familiar opening lines as I grabbed the remote and powered off the television.

If only I knew how true that would soon prove to be.

AJ

REBEL HEART

I wake up earlier than usual thanks to a random beep from somewhere in the house, immediately rolling over to snuggle into Brock...only he isn't there. What the fuck? Did he seriously bail on me in the middle of the night?

No. No, he wouldn't do that. Right? *Unless he already got what he was interested in* whispers the inner bitch in my mind. Maybe he's in another room? I tiptoe from the bed to the bathroom, naked as the day I was born, but when I swing open the door, he's not there.

I snag my robe from the hook on the door and slip it on as I trudge into the living room, feeling slightly defeated. Still no Brock. *What the fuck?* I continue into the kitchen and a piece of paper on the island grabs my attention.

Abs-

You can go ahead and stop with all those thoughts I know you're thinking. I didn't run out...did you really think you'd get rid of me that easily? Nah, get real firecracker. I have private golf sessions every Saturday and Sunday morning early AF. Sorry I forgot to tell you, please don't be mad. I'll call you when I finish up. Oh, and I made you a pot of coffee before I left.

-Brock

Ah! That's what the beep was—my coffee pot telling me it was finished brewing. My cheeks split into a wide grin as I pull a mug down from the cabinet, filling it with the nectar of the gods. I doctor it up just right and carry it back to my bedroom. Back in bed, I pull out my Kindle and skim through my TBR, finally settling on *Bashful*—a rom-com about a theater major who's majorly crushing on her bestie, who she assumes is gay.

I'm immediately sucked into this book, only pausing twice to refill my mug, and before I know it, *hours* have passed. Honestly, if it wasn't for my stomach growling and demanding food, I'd keep reading. After I power down my Kindle, I head into the kitchen in search of sustenance.

I settle on a peanut butter, jelly, and pretzel sandwich and an ice-cold glass of milk. Once I've cleared my plate, I check the time. It's almost noon, and I still haven't heard from Brock. While my irrational heart wants to panic, my logical brain reminds me he very well could still be golfing. Lord knows, when my dad went, he'd be gone for endless hours. Then again, for dear old dad, "I'm going golfing" roughly translated to "I'm out cheating with my secretary," so maybe not the best comparison.

I'm debating over whether or not I should text him when he calls me. Not caring about looking eager, I answer on the first ring. "Hey."

"Hey, Abs. You get my note?"

"I did. Thanks for leaving it. Not gonna lie, I was a little worried at first."

"Figured you might be. Sorry I forgot to tell you." I hear a car door shut in the background, followed by the sound of an ignition cranking. When he speaks again, his voice is low and husky. "I've been thinkin' about you all day—about last night...how hot you were."

His words light a fire in me, and I clench my thighs together. "I've been thinking about you, too."

"Oh yeah? Wanna tell me about those thoughts? In detail?"

"Are you trying to have phone sex with me while you drive?" I snort out a small laugh. "That doesn't seem safe."

"Good point, Abby Jane. Plus, why settle for your words when I get the real deal?"

"Oh, my God. You're so cocky."

"But I got the goods to back it." I'm about to ask him how he even fits in his truck with that ego of his, but he changes the subject. "Seriously, what are you up to today?"

"Other than wasting the day away in my bed reading, not much."

"West texted me earlier and asked if I wanted to go tubing in about an hour. You wanna come?"

"Yes!" My answer surprises me. I haven't been out to the river in a long time...in fact, I think the last time I went was the summer before Brock ditched me. But the thought of seeing him in his swim trunks outweighs my memories of our past—at least for today. "Can I invite Stacia?"

"For sure. I know West won't complain. I'll pick y'all up. Oh, and Abby Jane...I can't fucking wait to see you in a bikini."

The fact that Brock and I were both thinking about seeing the other in are swimsuits has me feeling giddy. I end the call and fire off a text to my bestie telling her to get her ass over here stat before dashing back to my room to get ready.

Thirty minutes later, I'm dressed in a pair of denim cutoffs and a white tank top, with my black two-piece swimsuit underneath. I'm sliding my feet into a pair of flip-flops when I hear Stacia let herself in. "Yo! You ready?" she hollers from the living room.

"Yup. Just packing a bag," I yell back, tossing a towel and some sunblock into my bag.

I walk out to where she is and find her raiding my fridge. "Fabulous. I grabbed us a six-pack on my way!"

"Nice. FYI, I need groceries, so your mission is a lost cause."

Stacia nudges the refrigerator closed with her hip. "Damn. I'm hungry."

"You know one of them will have food."

"Truth. Who all is going?" she asks, hoisting herself up to sit on my counter.

"I'm not sure. Brock and West are the only two I know for sure."

Stacia goes to reply, but my phone pings with an incoming text. "C'mon, he's here."

CHAPTER SEVENTEEN

BROCK

I pull up in front of Abby Jane's building and both West and I hop out to help the girls load up. "Just so you know, you're riding in the backseat."

"Are you being serious?" he asks, incredulous.

"As a heart attack. Plenty of room back there, Plus, Abby Jane invited her friend along."

West's interest is instantly piqued. "The hot one with the bull ring in her nose?" His question answers itself when the girls exit the building.

I swear to God, my mouth goes drier than the Sahara when my eyes land on Abby Jane. Her shorts are so short, they could pass as denim underwear, and I can see her skimpy black triangle top through her white tank. Having intimate knowledge of what that top is hiding, somehow makes it hotter. I reach down and adjust my hard-on as my girl approaches me.

She hesitates at the last second, so I step to her and take her beach bag from her. "Glad you decided to join us," I whisper the greeting before pressing my lips to hers, sucking on her bottom lip for a beat before pulling away. "Let's go. You've got shotgun."

She glances over to where West is helping Stacia load her drinks into the cooler—and by helping, I mean that he's staring at her ass as she bends over.

I snort at her unspoken question. "Yeah, I'm sure."

With everyone situated, I shift the truck into gear and pull out into the flow of traffic. "Hey, Brock," Stacia says. "Y'all have fun last night?" I catch her eyes in my rearview mirror, and she's smiling like the cat who ate the canary.

"More than you know." With one hand on the wheel, I reach out and grip Abby Jane's leg with the other, shooting a knowing look her way, causing her cheeks to pinken. Who knew I could make this little hardass blush so easily?

"Oh yeah? Wanna share details?" Stacia asks, and West groans beside her.

"I do not want to hear about my cousin's sex life." His comment strikes me as odd, because in the past he's had no trouble prying into my bedroom activities. I'll have to remember to ask him what's up when it's just the two of us.

"No. No details," Abby Jane answers for me. "What we do is between us."

"Spoilsport," Stacia grumbles, at the same time West says, "Thank God."

Abby Jane leans forward and fiddles with the radio until a song she likes comes on. We spend the rest of the drive listening to music, and I'm so zoned out, imagining her riding me the same way she's dancing in her seat, I miss our damn turn. "Shit," I mutter mostly to myself.

"What's wrong?" Abby Jane asks, laying her hand on my leg, dangerously close to my dick. *Just a little higher and to the left, firecracker.*

"Missed the turn."

"You did? Where?" She shifts in her seat, looking at the road behind us.

Her question is valid as fuck, because the only thing marking the dirt road turnoff is a little red reflector on a tree. I ride down a little farther until I can make a safe U-turn.

I nod toward the tree when we turn and Abby Jane shrugs. "Guess it's been a long time since I've been out here."

Stacia snorts. "No shit. Since like middle school, AJ. Wonder what made you wanna come today?"

"Probably the same person who made her come last night," West cracks, causing Stacia and me to laugh while Abby Jane to buries her face in her hands.

The road is long, winding, and riddled with potholes—making me extra thankful for my badass suspension. After about five minutes, we reach the outpost parking lot. I scan the dirt lot, looking for a spot my behemoth of a truck will fit into, because holy crap, there are a lot of people on the river today.

"Fuck," I curse out loud when I see a certain Benz parked in the shade next to the only open spot.

"Dammit." What in the hell is she doing here? This is *so* not her scene.

Abby Jane turns to face me, concern evident in her big, brown eyes. "What's wrong?"

West immediately spots what has me upset. "Sucks to be you, dude. Maybe she heard you'd be here?"

"Seriously," Abby Jane implores. "What's going on? She who?"

I suck in a breath through my teeth. "Amanda is here."

"Amanda as in…"

"Yeah. Her."

"Well, that sucks, but fuck her. She can only ruin our fun if we let her."

I can't help but grin at my girl's enthusiasm. "You know what? You're right, firecracker. Let's go."

The banks of the river are lined with dense woods, and every so often there's a sandbar perfect for breaking and eating. Abby Jane and I decided to share an innertube and no lie, floating under a cloudless sky with her body pressed against mine is the best form of torture. The tube with our cooler and waterproof radio is tethered to us and West and Stacia's tubes are tethered to it, leaving them far enough back that we can talk if we holler, but far enough that Abby and I have some semblance of privacy.

Though, not private enough for what's on my mind.

REBEL HEART

"Can we stop and eat soon?" Stacia yells over the music.

I shoot her a thumbs-up and as we approach the next sandbar, Abby Jane and I hop off of our float and help guide it to the bank. We fucking lucked out, because no one else is stopped here—it's just us and nature and the occasional sounds of other tubers passing by. West grabs the cooler, and Stacia produces a blanket from her bag. Once we get our stuff situated, we feast on cold fried chicken, pasta salad, and watermelon.

Stacia and West are goofing off in the water while we relax in the shade. I'm sitting with my legs out in front of me propped back on my elbows and Abby Jane is using my lap as a pillow. I'm so damn relaxed; this is truly shaping up to be the perfect Saturday until a cacophony of raised voices causes me to look up.

God, I wish I wouldn't have looked. Because sure enough, Amanda is walking my way, her hips swaying, but there's fire in her eyes. "Brocky!"

At the sound of her shrill voice, Abby Jane sits up and shoots me a look, silently asking if that's who she thinks it is. I give her a discreet nod. It's no wonder she doesn't recognize her, what with all the work Amanda's had: a new nose, filled lips, double D's, and then some—pretty fucking insane for a twenty-one-year-old.

"Hey there, Amanda. Didn't know you'd be out here today."

She frowns and inspects her perfectly manicured nails before replying. "Ugh. Me either. Rob said we were going out on the water. I thought he meant on a boat."

I hold back my snort, but Abby Jane…yeah, she doesn't.

Amanda turns her gaze to my girl. "You're Bill and Elenore's daughter?" Her lip curls in a nasty snarl.

Abby Jane though—she's cool as a cucumber. With a grace I didn't know she possessed, she rises from sitting to standing and extends a hand toward Amanda. "I am, and you are?"

This only serves to piss Amanda off even more. "Like you don't know who I am." She ignores Abby's outstretched hand, showing that she's not the polite socialite she'd have people believe her to be.

At this point, Stacia, West, and Rob—a new money douchebag—along with a few of his friends, are all making their way toward us from the water to watch the show.

Abby Jane drops her arm and silently scans Amanda from head to toe before frowning at her. "Honestly? I couldn't tell you from any other bitch on the avenue. Y'all are a dime a dozen and nothing to write home about. So, how about you step down off your pedestal and introduce yourself like a normal fucking person?"

Stacia starts to laugh, but West claps his hand over her mouth to silence her. Amanda stares at my firecracker in disbelief. "Brocky! Are you going to let that white trash Barbie talk to me like that?"

"I'm not her keeper; Abby Jane is a grown-ass woman. She can talk to you however she damn well pleases, but you best believe, you're gonna watch how *you* speak to *her*."

"Not to mention," Abs cuts in. "I'd rather be *trashy* than fucking fake."

Amanda scoffs at her but turns her focus back to me, a calculating gleam in her eyes. "Whatever. We're still on for dinner tonight, right?"

I know her aim was to piss Abby Jane off, but my firecracker sees right through her. "No, honey. He won't be eating with you tonight. He'll be eating me. Now, run along."

Rob steps forward, and I do too, thinking he's about to step up to my girl. Luckily, he's smarter than he looks; I relax when he wraps his hand around Amanda's wrist. "Come on, babe, let's go."

Thankfully she fucking listens.

CHAPTER EIGHTEEN

AJ

When Amanda and her stupid crew clear out, Brock walks over to me and crowds my space, running his hands down my sides and around my ass. Squeezing, he pulls me into him. "You were so fucking hot just then," he growls in my ear, causing chill bumps to dot my skin despite the sweltering heat.

"Yeah? You liked watching me tell that little twat off?"

Brock flexes his hips into mine, showing me just how much. "More than you fucking know."

West attempts to break through our lusty fog. "Y'all ready or what?"

Thank all the angels, Brock steals the words from my lips. "Nah, y'all untie from us and head on. We'll catch up."

"Whatever, dude."

Next thing I know, Brock is on me, nipping at my bottom lip, demanding entrance—which I immediately give. He kisses me until I'm weak in the knees. When we break apart, I notice Stacia left the blanket—she really is the best friend ever—and that gives me an idea.

With my mind made up, I snag the blanket up and grab Brock's hand, pulling him along behind me. "Where we going?" he asks.

I twist back to look at him and wink in lieu of a reply.

Once we're in the cover of the trees, I shake out the quilt and lay it on the ground before lowering myself down onto it. I crook a finger at Brock, indicating he should join me. "What are you doing, bad girl?"

"Anything I want," I whisper the words across his lips before I push him down onto his back, crawling into his lap and straddling him. I press my lips to his jaw, kissing my way down to his neck and then farther down his broad chest.

I'm almost to the promised land when Brock grabs me and hauls me back up so he can capture my lips with his. "Want you so bad, Abby Jane."

"Then have me." I whimper out the words.

He reaches up and slides the triangles to my top to the side before palming my breasts, testing their weight before pinching my nipples. Soon his tongue and teeth join his fingers, working me into a frenzy. I roll my hips over his hard length, desperate for friction. Unable to take his torture any longer, I reach down and untie the strings holding my bottom together.

Brock reads my intent loud and clear and taps my leg. "Raise up." I do, and he quickly shucks his swim trunks down his legs. "Birth control?" he asks, his tone like gravel.

"Yes," I moan, sinking down onto him. Brock lets me set the pace, and I take my time, working my hips in small, slow circles until we're both sweaty and writhing. Finally, he takes control and flips us so he's over me. He thrusts back into me, filling and stretching me. He sets a brutal, punishing pace, taking me right to the edge and into oblivion. The pressure is almost unbearable—right on the edge of pain but still deliciously good, and Brock keeps going, chasing both his release and mine.

"You feel so fucking good. So tight," he grunts as he hikes my right leg over his shoulder.

"God, yesss," I hiss as I crash over into white-hot, blinding pleasure. He follows right behind me, pulling out and finishing on my belly, with my name on his lips.

Brock rolls off to the side of me and pulls me into him. "Damn, Abs. Everything feels better with you. But I'm not gonna lie…I think I've got sand and dirt in places they got no business being."

I can't help but crack up at his words and our situation. Here we are, basically naked in the woods, with semen all over my stomach, while random people float down the river close enough that we can hear them as they pass. *Jesus*. What if someone would've wandered back here and stumbled upon us?

"Yeah. Safe to say we got a little wild. But" —I bite down on my lip— "I kind of like seeing you wild."

"It's all for you, firecracker."

I slide my top back into place and retie my bottoms.

"Good. Now give me something to clean up with."

Brock quickly pulls up his bottoms and looks around for something I can use. "Uh. Bad news Abby Jane…"

"Dammit!" I'll just use Stacia's blanket and wash it. Twice.

BROCK

By the time we get our float back on the water, the other tubers are long gone. It's just me, my girl, and nature. And with the sun starting to dip below the tree line, it's not quite as warm as it was when we started. Abby Jane shivers, and I pull her body closer to mine—well, as close as I can with the two of us and her bag all on one innertube—and rub my hand soothingly over her shoulder, trying to offer her some extra body heat.

"What time does the last trolley leave?" she asks, sounding sleepy.

"Around dusk."

"You think we're gonna make it?"

"Pretty sure. If I remember right, we should be almost finished."

And sure enough, as we crest the next bend, the little docking area comes into view. "Stay here, I'll hop off and guide us." I drop a quick kiss to her slightly sunburned cheeks and slide into the cool water. Once we're close enough to shore, I help Abby Jane off and the attendant finishes reeling in the raft.

I take her bag and heft it up over my shoulder before taking her hand in mine. We're the only people on the trolley back, and even though the drive is short, Abby Jane dozes off on my shoulder.

"Hey." I nudge her shoulder. "Gotta wake up, pretty girl. We're at the outpost."

She shakes her head, looking around. "Huh? Oh! We're back!"

"We are. C'mon. I'm sure West and Stacia are ready to read us the fucking Riot Act."

As we get closer to the truck, Abby Jane lets out a little laugh. "I don't know about that…I think they found something to do."

I follow her line of sight and see that my truck's rocking and the windows are fogged. "Oh, come the hell on. In *my* truck? Really?" Never in my life have I regretted giving my cousin a spare key more than I do right now.

I fight the urge to barge in, mainly because I don't want to see anything I can't *un*-see. Such as my cousin boning down with my girl's best friend. Abby Jane, however, has no such qualms and marches right over to the passenger side door and flings it open. *Jesus. They didn't even lock it?*

"Stacia Iris Kellan! Put your titties away and get off of his lap!" Abby Jane turns her back to face me, giving them a few moments to get situated. Two or so minutes later, Stacia calls out the all clear.

I help my girl into her seat before rounding the truck and climbing into my mine. Without looking back at my cousin, I say, "Not my truck. Anywhere but my fucking truck."

"We didn't—"

I cut him off. "Don't wanna know."

We settle in a mostly comfortable quiet. A quick glance at Abs and I see she's once again out cold. I check my rearview and see Stacia's asleep as well, with her head on West's shoulder.

"Seriously, dude, not cool."

"Nothing really happened. Well, no bodily fluids were exchanged."

"Swear to God, I'm gonna kill you," I grumble, turning up the radio to drown him out.

CHAPTER NINETEEN

AJ

It's been a few weeks since our tubing trip, and things with Brock are fucking amazing. Talk about words I never thought I'd say. But for once, I'm happy to be wrong. Because while *fuck yes,* I'm an independent woman, it feels good to have someone who truly gets me. The fact that he looks like a dream and dishes out orgasms like Costco does free samples doesn't hurt either.

Our free time, though limited, is spent together. If we're not grabbing a meal, we're studying…only now our study sessions are held at my apartment and typically end in my bed. Or the kitchen island. Sometimes the shower. Even against the wall a few times. Safe to say, studying has never been so fun.

Today, Brock is taking me golfing with him. While I don't particularly care for the sport, I'm excited to see him in his element. Plus, I bet his ass will look great in his khakis.

The question is, though, what on earth do I wear to play golf? Obviously most of my wardrobe isn't exactly country club appropriate, and while most days I don't give a fuck, I care about him and don't want to mess anything up for him.

After much debating, I finally settle on a somewhat modest black pleated skirt and a white polo I happen to have from high school—it's a bit snug, but not indecent. I slip on a pair of black knee socks and my black Converse…this is as good as it's going to get.

Brock told me to meet him around noon, so after a quick bite to eat, I'm out the door and on my way. It's one of those weird days where even though it's overcast and gray, it's bright as fuck. I rummage through my bag for my sunglasses and slip them on before exiting the building. It's so disgustingly humid that I'm sweating from making the short trek from my building to my car.

My car being black on black doesn't help things either. The hot leather of the seat stings my thighs and the steering wheel is almost too hot to grip. Nevertheless, I get my baby cranked and crack the windows before turning the air to full blast. I've finally cooled down just as I turn into the parking lot for the golf course… figures.

As I approach the clubhouse, I wind my hair up into a knot on the top of my head. In this sauna of a climate, I'll take comfort over cute any day. I'm about to head up the steps and go inside when two strong hands grip the dips in my waist from behind. A scream lodges itself in my throat, but I swallow it down when Brock's familiar, sexy scent envelops me.

I pivot around to face him and lightly smack his chest. "Holy fucknuggets! You scared the crap out of me!"

"Take a breath, firecracker." His voice is a deep rasp that hits me right between my thighs. "I didn't mean to. I just saw your fine ass over here looking like every naughty schoolgirl fantasy I've ever had come to life. I had to touch."

I can feel myself melting, and this time, it's not from the sun. "Well, warn a girl first next time, Jockstrap."

He pulls me a little closer, and thanks to the step I'm standing on, we line up perfectly for him to press a kiss to my lips, hard and fast and over way too quick. "C'mon, I've already got our token, so let's grab a bucket of balls and start at the driving range."

"I don't know what anything you just said means, but yeah, let's do it."

Brock chuckles and grabs my hand, leading me to what looks like a weird, squatty vending machine. I watch as he places a yellow basket in an opening at the bottom and then places his token into a little slot, much like the ones on arcade games. I jump when the machine starts clanging and shaking as it releases golf balls into his basket. He goes through the process a second time, leaving us with two buckets of balls to hit.

Balls in tow, Brock then guides me to the range. There are only two other golfers hitting balls right now—probably due to the stifling heat. We walk down to the far end where Brock's golf bag is already set up and waiting. Like a kid building a sand castle, he quickly flips the bucket upside down, careful to keep its contents inside. When he pulls the basket away, our balls are arranged in a neat little pyramid. Pretty fucking neat, if you ask me—not that I'd ever admit it.

"Tell me, Abby Jane, you ever swung a golf club?" he asks as he tugs a white leather glove onto his left hand.

Instead of answering his question, I ask one of my own. "You're right-handed; why is your glove on the left?"

"Noticed that, huh?" He brings his left out in front of him and flexes his fingers. While innocent, the motion still gives me shivers because I know exactly what those fingers can do. "Your glove goes on your top hand; it helps your grip."

"Weird."

"You're so damn cute," he murmurs as he boops me on the nose with his leather-covered index finger. "First things first: we need to stretch."

"Stretch? Like yoga?"

"Nothing that intense. Just to warm up. The kind of shit we did gym class." We work our way through a few poses and then Brock grabs a club from his bag. "This is a 9-iron. You typically use it when you're less than two hundred yards from the green. We're using it now because it is a good club to learn with.

"Downside, I'm a little taller than you, so you're gonna have to choke down on your grip. C'mere and I'll show you the proper way to hold it."

I walk over to him, and he moves behind me. He brings his arms around me, guiding them just below my own. "You want to start with your left hand." His voice is a husky murmur in my ear.

"Place it toward the top, almost like you're shaking hands with the club." He shows me what he means, holding his hand over mine.

"Then you're gonna wrap your right hand just below it, sliding your pinky into the space between your middle and pointer finger." He once again guides my movements, and I swear to God, his proximity has his words going in one ear and out the other. Seriously, how did we ever get any studying done at the start? It's like he bathes in pheromones fine-tuned for my libido. Even when he made me want to stab him, he was sexy as fuck.

"Abby Jane?" he says my name in a mildly exasperated tone, cluing me into the fact that he's probably had to say it more than once.

"Yes?" I bat my lashes, making myself the picture of innocence, which he promptly calls me on.

"You can take those fluttery lashes and shove 'em. We both know you're far too naughty to pull off the whole good girl act. And before you get offended, I fucking love it and wouldn't have you any other way." He swats my ass and carries on. "Now, as I was saying. We need to talk about posture and stance. Move your feet so they're shoulder-width apart and square your hips."

I try my best to do as he says, but my brain and my

body are *not* on the same wavelength. Maybe my brain has become a hussy and is in cahoots with my body, and this uncoordinated rebellion is all a ploy to get Brock's hands back on me.

"Here, let me show you." He trots over to his bag and grabs two more clubs, laying one at my feet with the head facing the range and the second parallel to it. "Okay Abby Jane, this first one is your target line." He kicks at my feet until they're properly spaced. "Remember your grip?" he asks, and I move my hands into the position he taught me.

"Good girl. Now we're gonna square these sexy hips of yours parallel to the target line." He wraps his hands around my hips and pulls them into the proper position.

"What next?" I ask breathlessly. Who knew golf could be so erotic?

"Now you're gonna address the ball." I let out a giggle.

"Not that ball, firecracker. Imagine there's a golf ball in front of your club. I want you to bend forward at the hips with your knees flexed a little—almost like you're holding a beach ball between them."

He runs a hand over my spine and my skin breaks out into gooseflesh. "Keep your back flat." I straighten my posture, rubbing my ass into his groin as I do. His voice is strained when he praises me. "Fuck. Just like that."

Once Brock is satisfied with my stance, he moves into working on my swing. He starts me with a small quarter swing, slowly working me up to a full one.

Watching his muscles flex and bulge, I can't take my eyes off of him as he demonstrates how to shift my weight for my backswing and my downswing. After a small eternity of practicing without a ball, Brock *finally* graduates me to the big leagues. We spend an hour driving balls down the range. Well, Brock drives them. Most of mine flop and roll, and on the off chance I manage to get one airborne, it either slices to the right or cuts to the left.

Eventually, I give up and decide to enjoy the view., a.k.a. Brock in the stance he worked so hard to teach me, swinging that club like he's fucking Arnold Palmer. After experiencing the viewing pleasure of Brock working through half of my basket and all of his, I can say with one-hundred percent certainty if all golfers looked like him, golf would totally be a spectator sport.

We're walking back to the clubhouse when I ask him, "What do you plan to do after you graduate?" And then it hits me—*holy shit. We've never talked about our majors. Not once.*

CHAPTER TWENTY

BROCK

Her question causes my steps to falter. We've talked about this, right? *Right?* I dip my head and cup the back of my neck. "Uh. I'm poli-sci."

Abby Jane blinks at me a few times. "Oh. Yeah. I guess that makes sense…" She trails off and nibbles her lip.

"What?" I can tell she wants to ask me something. Her wide eyes and fidgeting are a dead giveaway.

"It's just…is that what you want? To be a lawyer? To work for your dad?"

It's crazy how even after all these years she still knows me so well. "Why do you ask?" I keep my voice neutral, not wanting to give way to the emotion clogging my throat.

"I remember as a kid how much you hated the fact that your dad helped the bad guys escape jail time. And how sad his long hours made you and how upset you were when he missed birthdays, and…" She trails off again, and I'm struck speechless—because even though we drifted apart, my girl remembers almost everything about me.

"The all-out dream? The PGA Pro Tour. The sensible dream? I'd teach and run a golf camp for kids that can't afford a pro mentor. There's just something about giving back that feels good—about making a difference."

Abby Jane lets out this soft little sigh and steps closer to me, running her palm reverently over my jaw. "There's so much good in you, and my God, it's a turn on."

I'm tempted to lay my lips on hers and show her just how much *she* turns me on, but we're in public, in the middle of the clubhouse parking lot, so I rein it in. *Down boy*. "What about you, firecracker? You majoring in ass-kicking or what?"

"Actually, I have a double major: business and education with a concentration in literacy." She blushes when she says it, as if she's embarrassed by how fucking smart and dedicated she is.

"Really? That's cool as shit, Abby Jane. Do you know what you want to do with it?"

"You remember that recommendation letter I mentioned?"

"The one I used to blackmail you into not quitting as my tutor?" She smirks and narrows her eyes at me. "Yeah, I remember it."

"Well, Professor Doss helped kickstart Booking Out. It's a non-profit childhood literacy program. My goal is to get an internship and eventually transition to a full-time role."

"That's amazing." I press a chaste kiss to her lips. "You're amazing."

"Shut up," she says through a laugh. "What are you doing for the rest of the day?"

I heft my golf bag higher up onto my shoulder, causing the clubs to clank together. "Well…I was hopin' *you*."

Abby Jane flashes me a saucy grin. "That's an idea I can get behind."

"Wanna head to my place this time?" I ask, quickly adding that West isn't home.

"Yeah. I've never seen your space. I'll follow you there."

We each walk to our respective vehicles, and when she starts up her Chevelle, I have to smile. While my truck rumbles, her car roars—it's a freaking beast that could easily give my diesel a run for its money.

I check my rearview mirror every so often to make sure Abby Jane's still behind me. Sure, Cottonwood is small, and she would be able to find my place easily on her own, but I don't want to have to wait to get her under me. That short fucking skirt with those tall socks has been driving me insane all day.

Unfortunately, when I turn onto our street, I notice West's Mercedes in the driveway. *Dammit, he isn't supposed to be here.*

I throw my truck into park and kill the engine; Abby Jane meets me in the driveway. "I thought it was just gonna be us?"

"It will be," I reassure her. "C'mon."

Together, we set off for the side door, where I let us in. We kick off our shoes in the mudroom and set out to find West. The search is over quick, as he's in the kitchen at the island, hunched over his laptop. He startles when he hears us walk in. "Jesus—oh! Hey."

I raise a brow at him. "Didn't you have work today?"

"Ah. Decided to work from home." He sends my girl a wink and instinctively I pull her closer. He notices and laughs. *Fucker*.

"Well, maybe you should head to the office instead," Abby Jane tells him with a sweet smile.

"I'm being kicked out of my own house?" he asks, but his tone is joking.

Abby Jane walks over and pats his shoulder, like she's soothing a small child. "It's for your own good. Trust me."

West shakes his head with a small laugh. "Got it. Well, y'all have fun. Remember my motto, pleasure is momentary, babies are forever, so use protection."

He turns to walk out of the room, leaving his laptop behind. "Hey!" I holler after him. "Don't you need your computer?"

"Nah. Gonna call it quits. See if I can find me some afternoon delight. Think I'm in the mood for a redhead."

"You're such a fucking pig."

West winks. "Oink."

"So, you want a tour?" I ask once West is gone.

Abby Jane shrugs. "Sure. As long as it ends in your

bedroom."

As promised, the tour ends in my bedroom. She pauses in the doorway, taking in the space. Her eyes dart from the pale gray walls and thick crown molding to the wide-plank Brazilian hardwood floors. Aside from a few trophies, the room is undecorated. Hell, even my bedding is white. All in all, it's a boring room, but it gets the job done.

"What are you waiting for?" Abby Jane asks with a wicked gleam in her eyes as she steps fully into the room, pulling her white polo over her head as she moves.

I just about come in my pants when I catch a glimpse of her full tits encased in lavender lace. "Are you trying to kill me?" I croak out the words, blatantly ogling her chest.

"Noooo." She draws out the word. "I'm trying to fuck you."

Before I can recover to reply, she's unfastening her skirt and sliding it down her legs, leaving her in nothing but her matching lingerie set and tall, black socks. Her attire, much like her, is the perfect contradiction. Sugar and spice, and oh my goddamn, everything nice.

She's tough as nails but still soft and vulnerable. She's an open book and an enigma. She's rough edges and a soft center. And she's all fucking mine.

And right now, she's sinking to her knees, looking up at me like she wants to swallow me whole. *Who the hell am I to deny her?* I move to undo my belt, but she knocks my hands out of the way. "Let me." She expertly unbuckles it before sliding the leather through the loops, pulling it off entirely. She fumbles a bit with the double closure of my khakis, but still gets them undone and pushed down in what has to be record time.

The minute her warm, wet mouth envelops me, I start reciting golf stats in my head to keep this ecstasy from ending too soon. But it's no use. My girl works me like a pro, and all too soon, I'm tapping her cheek to let her know I'm about to blow so she can pull away. But true to her nature, Abby Jane keeps going, sucking me down until I have nothing left to give.

She licks her lips and hums as she pulls away, and I swear, my knees go a little weak. "You are so fucking perfect." I offer her my hand and help pull her to standing before mashing my lips to hers, loving the way I taste on her tongue.

I walk us back toward my bed until her thighs hit my mattress. Knowing exactly what I want, Abby Jane crawls up onto my bed, situating herself in the center. I kiss my way up her body, starting at the top of her tall socks, pausing in all the right places until she's worked up to panting, and I'm ready to go again.

We spend what feels like hours lost in each other's bodies, and while it's certainly not anywhere near our first time, something's different. We're less fevered. We both take our time, exploring and touching. I learn that if I tug the metal in her nipples while I'm inside her, it's a hot-button guaranteed to set her off like a bomb. And she learns that raking her teeth over my hipbone is a surefire way to get me hard enough to split wood.

We're insatiable, and I fucking love it…I love her.

Oh fuck.

I totally fucking love Abby Jane Adams. Like, *take my balls and nail them to the wall because I'm so lost over this girl* love her. The question is, does she feel the same?

CHAPTER TWENTY-ONE

AJ

It's been a few weeks since our golf date—slash—mind-bending, life-changing, record-setting sex-a-thon. Though, if I'm being honest, it was so much more than sex…for me, at least. That afternoon, Brock Larson moved mountains and broke down every wall that surrounded my heart.

It was also the day I realized I was head over fucking heels in love with him.

Only, since then he's been sketch-city—acting cagey as hell. He says it's because his coach has upped their practices from fifteen to twenty hours a week. And that's on top of his volunteer hours, classes, and private sessions.

So, I get that he's crazy busy, but none of that explains why he's on his phone more than usual or why he's been so tense and stressed. For once my heart and my brain aren't at war; my emotional side says he's hiding something from me, and my logical side fucking agrees.

He's blown off our last two study sessions, and it

wouldn't surprise me if he canceled our plans for tonight either. I keep trying to reassure myself that we're fine, but with us hardly talking, the nagging feeling in my gut won't shut up. It screams that I'm losing him. That shit got too serious, and he's distancing himself from me—from us—and dammit, it hurts.

In need of a second opinion, I text Stacia.

Me: Come over. Please.

Me: 911.

Stacia: Give me fifteen. Love you. Will bring coffee.

I'm wearing a trail through the living room rug when Stacia lets herself in, just a short knock announcing her arrival. "What's wrong, AJ?"

"Nothing." I pace back and forth. "Everything. I don't know."

Stacia moves farther into the room and sets the two beverages she's holding onto the coffee table before plopping down onto my couch. She pats the seat beside her. "Come. Let's talk. I don't like seeing this stressy-messy side of you."

I let out a deep sigh and take a seat next to her. She promptly hands me an extra-large iced coffee, which I greedily suck down, hoping an extra dose of caffeine will soothe all that ails me.

"Brock's being weird, and it has me crazy."

"Weird how?" she asks, assessing me over the lid of her cup.

"Weird like...like he's about to ghost me."

"Girl. Please. I'm pretty sure that man loves you."

I snort, but it's sad sounding. "Doubtful. You haven't been around us lately. He's distant, and I hardly see him, which I get—I do. He's busy with golf, but he's even skipped our last two study sessions. When we *are* together, he's glued to his phone. I'm talking full-on extension of his arm. The only time he's his normal self is when we're fucking." I run my hands through my unruly hair. "I've been waiting all day for him to cancel our plans tonight."

"I can see how that would be problematic. Now, don't slap me for asking, but have you talked to him?"

I deflate at her question, because to an extent, she's right. I haven't outright asked him anything. Maybe tonight I will. You know, if he doesn't bail.

"Tell ya what...you go take a bubble bath, and I'll pick you out a killer outfit, and then I'll do your hair and makeup, okay?"

"Okay. Love you, bitch."

"Love you right back. Now, go!"

BROCK

I know Abby Jane can tell something's off with me. At first, it was me processing the realization that I love her. Then it morphed into my wanting to make sure the first time I told her was nothing less than perfect. But now…now it's more complicated.

"Brock!" my dad barks out my name like he's a drill sergeant.

"Yes, sir?" I've been at the house for hours, going round and round in circles with him over my post-grad plans. Trying to get him to see my perspective is like talking to a rock.

He stalks over to where I'm seated in his office and thrusts a stack of papers in my face. "You're going to apply to Emory! You're going to follow in my goddamn footsteps! And you're going to do it with a smile on your face. You should be grateful for the path I've paved for you. Here's your future on a silver platter, and you're dumb and naïve enough to pass it up."

His face is beet red and sweat beads his hairline. If he were animated, smoke would be billowing out of his ears. "I'm not naïve, Dad."

"And for what?" he bellows, steamrolling right over me like I hadn't even opened my mouth. "To teach? To play golf? To give back? Get real, son! If you want to give back so badly, do as I say and make charitable contributions. I will tell you right now, though, no son of mine is going to waste his potential on my dime."

He huffs out a breath as if trying to regain his composure. I'm about to take him down a peg when he starts back up, effectively cutting me off. "Not to mention, I've heard you're gallivanting all around with

Abby Jane." He spits her name like a curse and I see red. "I'd say dating her is charity enough."

My fury propels me forward from the couch, causing him to take a step back. "Don't you dare talk about her like that. Don't you even fucking say her name. She's the best damn thing to ever—"

But Dad's not having it, and he roars over me. "She is a disgrace. A bad apple. And I forbade you from seeing her!"

"You forbade me? Get real, old man. I'm a grown-ass man, and I'm capable of making my own decisions—your input's not wanted or—"

My words are cut off when his fist crashes into my jaw. The force of the blow causes me to lose my footing, and I crash back into the couch.

"She's not meant for you. She's not good enough for the Larson name and I won't have you disgrace our family any more than you have." He moves in closer to where I'm slumped against the sofa, hand gripping my throbbing face. "You will fall in line Brock, or there'll be consequences."

I scramble up from my prone position and charge toward the door. "That's right, Brock. Run." I'm almost to the door when he calls out to me again. His words—full of menace and dark intent—send dread snaking through my veins. "And be sure to have a good time tonight."

He's lost his goddamn mind if he thinks he has a say in who I date. And tonight, I plan to show my girl just how much I love her—his threats be dammed.

CHAPTER TWENTY-TWO

AJ

Stacia left twenty minutes ago, after she finished dolling me up, in order to give me some time to get my head on right, so to speak. I'm seated at the foot of my bed, decked out in a form-fitting little black sheath dress with a floral lace overlay and a halter neckline. It's demure and sexy all at once. Stacia suggested pairing the dress with black stilettoes, but I opted for nude pumps instead.

I gave her free rein on my hair and makeup. She styled my faded, barely-there pink locks in voluminous, beachy waves and complimented them with a fresh-faced look—subtly winged liner to make my brown eyes pop, rosy cheeks, and nude lips. All in all, I look pretty…tame. But pretty, nonetheless.

Maybe a glass of wine will help scatter this stupid melancholy mood that's been hovering over me like a dark cloud. Maybe it'll take the edge off.

I trudge from my bedroom to the kitchen and fling my fridge open, reaching for the blue bottle of Riesling. It's already uncorked, so I don't bother with a bottle opener, instead pulling the stopper out with my teeth before guzzling two gulps straight from the bottle.

I'm moving in for my third swig when there's a knock at my door. I check the time—seven on the dot. Guess Brock's here. I recork the bottle and shove it back into the fridge. On the way to the door, I take one last fortifying breath before opening it and coming face-to-face with the man I love—who may not love me.

Momentarily, I'm struck speechless. I've seen Brock dressed up a thousand times growing up—from cotillion to school dances, but none of those moments hold a candle to now. I start at the bottom, taking in his shiny black dress shoes and tailored charcoal pants. His black button down is stretched snugly across his muscled chest, and his hair's gelled back and away from his face. I gasp when I see his left eye—all swollen and black and blue, the only thing marring his otherwise perfect appearance.

"Oh, my God! Brock, are you okay?" I lift my hand to touch it but think better of it and let it fall back down to my side. "What happened?"

Brock shrugs off my concern. "No big deal, firecracker. I wasn't paying attention and walked into someone's backswing."

I'm not sure if I believe him, but I decide to let it go. He moves closer to me and wraps his arms around me, burying his face in my neck. "I've missed you so much, Abby Jane. So fucking much."

His warm breath tickles my neck, and I lean into

him a little more. "I've missed you too." He steps back from me and reaches out and fingers one of my curls. "I'm sorry I've been so distant. Shit's gonna get better, I swear it."

I smile widely at his proclamation. Maybe tonight will be exactly what we need to get back on track. "So, what's for dinner?" I ask, giving him an out.

Brock links his arm with mine and guides me toward the elevator. "I made us reservations at The Colony Grill."

My mouth waters. "Oh, I haven't eaten there in forever!" We spend the drive there in a companionable silence, simply taking comfort in one another's presence. Brock pulls into the valet line and shifts his truck into park before exiting the vehicle. The attendant opens my door for me, but Brock waves him out of the way and helps me down himself.

We step into the restaurant, and I'm instantly hit with waves of nostalgia. Memories of Mother's Day brunches and family dinners flit through my mind. I waste no time shutting that vault—now's neither the time nor the place for an impromptu trip down memory lane.

"Good evening and welcome to The Colony Grill," the hostess greets us. "Do y'all have reservations with us tonight?"

"We do," Brock tells her. "Two under Larson."

She frowns and taps around on her touchscreen for a few seconds. "Oh! Yes. There you are. Sorry, we have another—never mind. Not important. Your table is ready. If you'll follow me?" She grabs two menus and fans her free hand out Vanna White style.

We trail behind her, weaving our way through the dimly lit space, passing patrons enjoying their romantic, candlelit dinners. She leads us back to a small, round table located in the middle of the dining room.

Ever the gentleman, Brock pulls out my chair for me before seating himself. "Harrison will be y'all's server this evening, and he'll be with y'all shortly. Thank you so much and have a great meal." She places our menus on the table before turning and walking back the way she came.

Inexplicably, the fine hairs all over my body stand on end and the back of my neck and ears feel hot—you know, that feeling you get when you're being watched. I quickly scan the room, but I don't see any familiar faces. *How odd.*

"What sounds good to you, Abby Jane?" Brock asks, and it takes everything in me not to answer with *you.* I've missed him so much, but my Spidey senses are tingling, telling me tonight might change everything—I can only hope it's for the better.

Scanning the menu, I take my time replying. "I'm thinking the seafood risotto. I love scallops. You?"

I sweep the restaurant again. But still, nothing. "Mmm. That does sound good. Think I'm gonna get the shrimp and grits."

Our server comes by to greet us, and we go ahead

and place our order. Moments later, another server deposits a basket of rosemary rolls along with two plates. I help myself to one, sighing as the flavors burst across my tongue.

I move to get a second roll when my stomach clenches with nerves. Quietly, I excuse myself to the restroom. I desperately need to get a grip. All night, it's felt as though someone has been watching me, but I'm pretty sure I'm just projecting my own paranoia about my relationship with Brock, and it's making me fucking crazy.

Inside the restroom, I close myself into a stall, even though I don't actually have to *go*. I just need a moment to breathe—a moment to get my emotions under control. After a few deep breaths, I'm ready to head back out to my table. As I'm opening the stall door, a beautiful, curvy blonde breezes in, setting up shop in front of the sink.

Not paying her much attention, I place my clutch on the countertop and turn on the faucet, lathering my hands, when the blonde turns to me. "Hello there, Abigail."

I tilt my head to face her and suck in a breath through my teeth. "Amanda, right?" *What are the fucking chances she's here at the same time Brock and I are here?*

"Oh, honey." Amanda coos the words like I'm a child. "I simply cannot let this charade go on a moment longer."

"Wh-what charade?"

She places her left hand across her heart and the shiny oval diamond she's sporting glints in the mirror. "You and Brock."

Her words and condescending tone sparks fury within me. "I don't know who the fuck you think you are—"

Amanda cuts me off. "His future wife is *who the fuck I am,* as you so crudely put it." She wiggles her left hand in front of my face. "See this ring? It was his Mimi Jean's. I know you think y'all have something, and goodness, maybe y'all do. But here's the thing—he was promised to me. His daddy and my daddy made a deal a long time ago, and I'm not going to let your white-trash-fallen-from-grace-skank-ass ruin my future."

My mind races, desperately trying to make sense of her words. She steps closer to me, backing me into the marble countertop. "I know this hurts, honey, but it's the truth. I know it. Brock knows it, and now, you know it. He and I had an agreement. I told him he could go and sow his wild oats before we settled down, but playtime is over."

My eyes sting, but I hold my tears back, unwilling to cry in front of her. "I-I don't believe you."

Her lips twist into an ugly scowl. "God, you're pathetic. Has he been acting different lately? He has, hasn't he? Wanna know why? He brought you here to end things. He planned on doing it right after dinner. I've been waiting at the bar so I could join him for dessert."

No. No-no-no-no. There's that favorite word of mine, only right now it's failing me, because everything she's saying makes *so much* sense. I mean, aside from a hug when he picked me up and helping me down from his truck, he hasn't touched me at all tonight. We haven't seen each other in days, and he didn't even try to steal a kiss.

Surprise, surprise! Brock Larson is exactly who I thought he was from the start, and the bastard knowingly made me fall for him just so he could fuck me over in the end. Talk about the story of my life. The only man who's never let me down is my gramps, but at the end of the day, the only person to blame for this is me.

I let him back into my life. I let him into my bed. I let him into my heart. But now…now I'm going to rid my life of him entirely. "You know what, Amanda?" I calmly grab my clutch as I move her away from me and step toward the door. "Y'all deserve each other. Have a nice life."

I rush out of the restroom, making a beeline straight to the exit. As soon as the muggy evening air hits my face, I let the tears fall. I move away from the restaurant as fast as my heels will carry me, finally slumping down onto a park bench a good two blocks away.

With trembling hands, I fish my phone out of my clutch and order an Uber. Five minutes later, I'm sitting in the backseat, silently weeping the entire ride back to my apartment, tears rolling down my cheeks and off of my chin. I can only imagine how crazy I look, but I can't find it in me to care.

The driver idles in front of my building, and I grab what little cash I have in my clutch and give it to him as a tip. With every step I take the soft silk of my dress—the one I wore especially for him—burns like acid as it rubs against my skin. I rip it off as soon as I'm safely locked inside my apartment, and like the pathetic girl I've somehow let myself become, I slip into one of Brock's shirts.

I bring it to my nose and inhale; his scent sets off a fresh round of tears as I sink down onto my bed, burying myself in the comforter and my grief.

CHAPTER TWENTY-THREE

BROCK

Abby Jane's been in the restroom for what feels like forever. And I'm not even exaggerating. I've already had my drink refilled and a second basket of bread brought out.

I'm about to go and check on her when Amanda fucking Burkett slides into my girl's vacant chair. "The fuck do you want?" I snarl at her.

She blinks slowly at me before breaking out into a beaming smile. "Brocky! That's no way to speak to your future wife."

Her words cause me to choke on thin air. "My what, now?"

Not missing a beat, the little psycho reaches across the tabletop and takes my hand in hers. It's then I notice she's wearing my fucking grandmother's ring. "Where the fuck did you get this?" I growl, trying to pull my hand away from hers, but she digs her nails in.

"Oh, Brocky." She shakes her head like she feels sorry for me, but who she needs to worry about is herself, because if she's the reason my girl's not back, she's gonna fucking feel my wrath. "You're being so silly. You knew this was the plan. You've known all along that I'm the only future you have."

I yank my hand back, knocking my glass of water off of the table in the process. I shove my chair back and jump to my feet. "What did you do? Where is Abby Jane?"

Amanda laughs lightly, like I've just delivered a witty one-liner. "I ran into her in the restroom and sent her home. She understands now, Brocky. I did your dirty work for you, baby." She stands as well and steps closer to me. At this point, other patrons are staring, watching the shitshow unfold.

"You did what? You fucking bitch! You had no fucking right—"

"You will watch how you speak to me!" she shrieks. "You will respect me. I'm not some two-bit whore. I'm a lady, and you will treat me as such!" She pinches the bridge of her nose and takes a deep breath. In a much calmer voice, she continues speaking. "She needed to know, Brocky. You're mine—you've always been mine. You were promised to me, and I'm ready to collect. I'm ready to build our future—"

Over her shit and all of the insanity flowing from her pastel pink lips, I flag down a passing server and slip him two crisp hundred-dollar bills. "This should cover everything. I'm so sorry for all of the trouble." With the bill taken care of, I step around Amanda, but she follows behind me, hot on my heels.

REBEL HEART

I burst through the door and out onto the sidewalk. Unfortunately, I have to wait on the valet to bring my truck around, which gives Amanda the perfect opportunity to keep spewing her bullshit at me. "Don't you walk away from me, Brocky! We are *not* finished! Brock! Are you listening to me?"

Unable to listen to her drivel for another second, I spin to face her, a menacing look on my face. "Are *you* listening to yourself? You sound fucking crazy. We're not together. We've never been together, and we never will be. You need to stop this nonsense."

"My future isn't nonsense!" Her voice wobbles, but I can't find it in myself to feel sorry for. This girl needs serious help. "You are mine. *Mine!* Why can't you just fall in line?"

Those last three words cause me to freeze in place. *Fall in line*. The exact same thing my father said to me earlier today. Oh, my God. How did I not fucking see this?

As soon as the realization hits me, my truck is ready. I rush the attendant, snatching my keys. I peel out like a bat out of hell, leaving Amanda sputtering on the sidewalk.

I dial my mother the second my phone connects via Bluetooth. "Brock, honey, how are you?"

I skip over all pleasantries and get down to business. "Did you know?" The anger in my tone is unrestrained, and for a split second, I feel bad—I've never spoken to my mother like this, but the thought of her being a part of this guts me.

"Did I know what? Honey, what's going on? What are you talking about?"

She sounds sincere, but I'm hesitant. "Did you give Amanda Burkett Mimi Jean's ring?"

"Absolutely not. It's safe and sound in my jewelry box—where it will remain until you settle down with the only woman worthy of it." Her tone leaves no room to argue. She truly had no prior knowledge of this—thank God. My mom has always been even-keeled, and I'm relieved as fuck to know that hasn't changed.

"You might want to double check," I inform her angrily.

I hear rustling through the speakers. "Oh, my word!" she exclaims. "Where? How?" I listen as she connects the dots. "He wouldn't. That dirty, no good bastard!"

I smirk at her foul language, as it's so unlike her. "He did. I just had the damn ring flashed in my face."

"That conniving little witch—just like her mother."

"It gets worse. All of this came after she ran Abby Jane off."

"Oh, honey. We will work this out. You head home, and in the morning, come by and we will start putting out fires. In the meantime, I'm going to have a very serious talk with your father."

The thought of her confronting him worries me. Just because he's never laid a hand on her yet doesn't mean he won't. "Wait for me and we will confront him together tomorrow."

REBEL HEART

"Oh, I can handle your father."

I pull into my driveway and slam the gear shifter into park and hesitate, wondering if I should tell her about him decking me. Quickly, I realize she absolutely has the right to know. "Mom, please wait. Today in his office he punched me, and he back-handed me the other day."

My confession is met with stark silence followed by a sharp intake of breath. "He. Did. What?" The fire in her tone shocks me. She's always seemed too meek and mild, but this woman now is a fucking dragon. "I will end that man, Brock. No one—and I mean *no one*—lays their hands on my boy and gets away with it."

"It's okay, Mom. I can handle him."

Mom laughs darkly. "Oh, honey. I know you think I let him walk over me, but here's the truth…I don't love your father. I married him because our fathers arranged it and held some things over my head. The only good thing to come out of our sham of a union is you. You are my heart and my joy. And he's gone too far this time. I know I've let you down, honey, but I'll fix this. I love you." She ends the call before I can say another word.

I dial Abby Jane's phone, but she never answers—not that I expected her to. Even still, I call her a few more times, finally settling on leaving a voicemail begging her to call me, begging her to let me explain.

Pissed beyond words, I storm into the house, only

to find West with some random girl humping him like a dog on the couch. I loudly clear my throat, and he dislodges his tongue from her mouth long enough to catch my eye.

When he sees the anger in my stare, he stills her ever-moving hips. "Time to go, sweetheart."

She balks. "Are you kidding me? God! You really are an asshole."

He tsks her. "Family first, doll."

She storms out of the house in a huff, but West looks totally unaffected. He nods to the cushion next to him, gesturing for me to have a seat—*hell no, not happening.*

"Kitchen," I grunt. "I need a drink." I snag two cold beers from the fridge and lean back into the counter.

"What's up?"

"Fucking everything." I launch into the events that led to tonight, detailing everything out for him—from realizing I love Abby Jane, to my dad, to Amanda's crazy self. By the time I'm finished, his jaw is damn near on the floor.

"So, whatcha gonna do?"

"Fuck if I know. What can I do? At this point, Abby Jane isn't answering my calls…not that I blame her. I wouldn't either."

"You tried going by her place?"

I shake my head. "Nah. As much as I want to storm the castle, so to speak, I know it wouldn't get me anywhere—except shanked. She would probably kill me."

"Truth." We both take a moment and polish off our beers. "Well, you can only fight one battle at a time, so let's start with that douche-ant you call Dad."

"I wanna fucking kill him," I say honestly. "I'm talking cold-blooded murder."

"Can't let ya do that—especially since you just made my ass an accessory." He chortles at his own joke. "But what I can do is help you come up with a plan to fix this shit."

"But how? How can I fix this? You know how stubborn Abby Jane is. She's not going to willingly talk to me."

"And that's where I come in. You worry about sorting shit out with your dad, and I'll worry about getting you and your girl in the same room."

The minute the sun rises, I'm out the door and on my way to my parents' house. I'm running on no sleep, a bad attitude, and too much alcohol—but this can't wait another second. Hell, if I would've had my way, I'd have been here last night, but I respect my mom enough to let her have at him first.

On the drive over, visions of a future without Abby Jane by my side assault me. Sure, I messed shit up between us in middle school, but deep down, I know I've always loved her—that she's always been the one for me. And, finally, I got a second chance, only for life to shit all over it.

She's the splash of color in my world, and I'm not letting her go this time around. I'll fight for her—for us—as long as it takes. Until I'm fucking blue in the face. Abby Jane is meant for me and I won't stop until she sees what I already know.

I storm up the steps and pound on my front door. I'm shocked when Mom answers the door instead of Marta. She glances over her shoulder and steps out onto the porch.

"What's going—"

"Oh, honey. I have a plan."

"You do?" I ask, wondering just what she has up her sleeve.

"Yes. You're gonna go inside and confront your father, and I'm going to film it from the hall. I won't tell you what to say or how to act, but to an extent, play along."

"Play along?" I whisper-shout, outraged. *Why would she fucking suggest this?*

"I know it sounds crazy, but your father is well-respected in our community, and if we're not careful, he'll take us down with him, honey."

"Do you really think it will work? That it will be worth it?"

Mom pauses, choosing her words carefully. "He's a snake, Brock. I think it's the only way. No one would ever believe what he's really like, so we need to show them his true colors."

I don't know if I totally approve of this plan, but

REBEL HEART

reluctantly I agree, and we head inside.

"Your father is in his office. Head on back."

I do as she says, feeling all kinds of conflicted about her plan. But at the end of the day, I have to trust her.

I rap my knuckles on the open door of the office and step inside. "Brock," my dad sneers. "Why are you here?"

"We need to talk." It's a struggle to keep my tone even when all I want is to throttle him.

"Come to your senses?"

"About what?" I ask, stepping farther into the room. "About my major?"

"Among other things."

"Other things like the fact that you're trying to force me into marrying Amanda Burkett?"

He replies with a humorless laugh. "Force is a strong word, son."

"Yet so accurate, because here she is with a ring on her finger that I didn't give her. Where did she get it, Dad?"

"That hardly matters. You act like marrying her would be a hardship. Tight little body like hers? I know I wouldn't complain."

I wish I could say his words shock me, but they don't. He's always been a fucking dog. "I don't love her. I'll never love her."

"Love has nothing to do with it!" He screams the words so loudly my ears ring.

"So, you're saying you don't love Mom?"

"You truly are naïve, son. Your mother was a stepping stone. I wanted a certain type of lifestyle, and she had the purse strings to provide one. Didn't hurt that she spread her legs for me like a whore. Unfortunately, that led to you." He spits the words at me, and I'm shaking with barely concealed rage.

"You disgust me."

As soon as the words pass my lips, his fist slams into my face, sending me onto my ass. "Likewise. But here's the thing, son. You're *going* to do as I say, or you can kiss this comfortable lifestyle goodbye."

I rub a hand over my cheek before hefting myself up from the floor. My anger turns to incredulity, because what the fuck is he even talking about? He's acting like he foots the bill for my life, but that's a fucking joke. I live—very comfortably, I might add—off of a trust from my Mimi Jean and have a full ride to school. I fight the urge to set his ass straight since Mom asked me to play along.

"It's like that?" I ask him, trying my best to sound scorned.

"Yeah, son. It is."

"I see. I guess my hands are tied then, huh?"

At my compliance, it's like he's a totally different person. Fucking split personality or some shit. "I don't want to force anything, but promises and plans have been made, and you need to fall in line."

Jesus, he's insane. But there are those three words again. I grind my molars together and give him a terse

REBEL HEART

nod.

"Good boy. I knew you'd come around. Now, next Friday night, Hal Burkett and I have planned an engagement party for you and Amanda at the clubhouse. Be there no later than half past six."

It fucking kills me to smile and agree, but I do because surely Mom has a plan that will work.

CHAPTER TWENTY-FOUR

AJ

The past week has been nothing short of pure misery. Everything fucking hurts, and my mood is piss and vinegar.

My heart hurts from losing Brock.

My pride hurts from being so easily fooled.

My body hurts from hiding out in my bed anytime I'm not in class.

My head hurts from crying so much.

I've never in my entire life felt more pitiful than I do now. I've always thought I was strong, but this has proved that I'm not.

Then again, maybe I'm not giving myself enough credit. I've at least been strong enough to ignore his calls. The Saturday after everything went down, he called at least every other hour—to ease his guilty conscience, I assume.

Sunday, he only called four times.

Monday and Tuesday, he only called twice.

Wednesday and Thursday, only once.

And today…nothing. Nada. Zip. Which I guess

means things are really and truly over. Stacia has been on me relentlessly to either answer or call him back. She's adamant that there's more going on than what it seems, but I call bullshit.

Even though she thinks I'm doing myself a disservice by not hearing him out, Stacia has been my rock this week. She's like my very own fairy godmother. Every morning she shows up with a coffee, some type of pastry, and a pep talk. And every night she brings me dinner, and we watch some sort of girl-power movie.

I've always known she was the best bitch on this planet, but this week has shown me she's so much more amazing than I thought. She doesn't push me to talk about Brock, other than raising her brow at me when I don't answer.

But tonight, she says we have plans and that I've moped long enough.

"AJ?" Stacia yells my name as she lets herself into the house.

"Bedroom," I holler back.

She flounces into my room not even two seconds later, her arms loaded down with shopping bags. "Get out of bed. We have plans."

I sink deeper into my plush bedding. "Do we have to?"

She scrunches up her nose as she takes in my rumpled appearance. "Yes. We very much do. Seriously, get up. I booked us at the salon."

At this I perk up—after all, a little pampering certainly can't hurt. In fact, I'd say it's just what the doctor ordered.

I amble into my closet and come back out dressed in cropped yoga leggings and an oversized T-shirt. "Ready."

"Great. Let's go." She starts for the door, but then stops and turns back to me. "Oh! Give me your phone. Today's about us." Begrudgingly, I do as she says.

Stacia drives us across town to Color Me Crazy—our salon of choice. "Any idea whatcha want done?" she asks me as she whips her little coupe into a spot in front of the shop.

"I dunno yet. I've been toying with the idea of adding some purple. We'll see. What about you?"

With a waggle of her brows, she says, "As blonde as possible. Maybe even silver."

"Ooh!" I clap my hands together. "Yes! Do that!"

We enter the funky little salon, which is housed in two pink-painted shipping containers that have been welded together. Music is pumping through the speakers, loud enough to be heard over the whirring of the hair dryers. So loud, in fact, the receptionist has to raise her voice to speak to us.

Once we enter the main area, it's a little quieter, but I'm not complaining either way. "Hey girl!" Alessia, my stylist, greets me. "Long time no see!"

I plop down into her chair, eager for her to work

her magic. "The perks of being a natural blonde. But…I want to change it up today."

"Okay. Tired of the pink?"

"No. I just…it's time for a change." I twist my fingers together. "New hair, new me, right?"

"Girl. You are fabulous as is. So, why are you looking for a 'new you?'"

I heave out a deep sigh. "Just a lot going on, and I need a pick me up."

"I can get behind that. Let's talk—whatcha wanna do?"

"I'd show you a picture, but Stacia's confiscated my phone."

Alessia fishes her phone out of her apron pocket and asks me what to search for. A few taps and swipes later, she's gushing about my proposed new look. "Girl! No lie, I pinned this *exact* pic last night. Oh-em-gee! I'm so excited!"

Four hours later, Stacia and I are all finished—me with a root-y ombre that fades from a dark purple to shades of pink, giving way to almost translucent white ends, and Stacia with a pretty silvery hue.

"What next?" I ask, because knowing her, our day is just beginning.

"Mani and pedis. Duh."

By the time we make it back to my apartment, I've been waxed, plucked, scrubbed, masked, and moisturized within an inch of my life. I swear to God, I could put a gold-medal-winning show dog to shame in the primping department right about now.

"Now we can relax?" I ask with a hopeful tone. "Maybe eat some ice cream, watch some *PLL*?"

"No can do, bit-chacho." I give her a toddler-worthy whine and shoulder shimmy, but Stacia ignores my antics. "We have plans tonight and going is non-negotiable. Sorry, not sorry."

All I offer her in return is a blank stare. But she's in no mood to deal with my shit. "C'mon, AJ. Time to get you lookin' extra pretty."

"Do I have to dress up?" I really don't want to dress up. As stupid and immature as it is, the last time I got all gussied up, I found out that the love of my life viewed me as nothing more than a hot little premarital rebellion.

"You absolutely do. And I get to pick your outfit."

"And let me guess…you also get to do my makeup?"

"Look at you, ya smart cookie. Now, hush up and lemme work."

Forty-five minutes later, Stacia has me contoured and highlighted to the nth degree. My eyes are slicked with a shimmery gold shadow, and my lips are a bright fuchsia. All in all, I look way hotter than I feel.

"Now, let's get you dressed."

"You wanna tell me where we're going?"

"Not really, nope." *Ugh. Figures.*

She rifles through the shopping bags she brought

with her and pulls out a stunning velvet dress in the most spectacular dusty rose color. "Here. Put this on."

I know I won't get my way, so I don't bother arguing. I slip the material over my head and check my reflection in the mirror. I'm not sure what our plans are, but this dress will certainly turn heads. The fabric hugs my body like I'm sewn into it—undies and a bra will for sure be a no-go. It hits mid-thigh and sports a deep vee with straps so thin they may as well be dental floss.

Oh. *Oh, no.* Maybe turning heads is part of her plan. What if she's planning to parade me around at some club in hopes of finding me a rebound hook-up? *Oh, God. I feel sick.* I don't think I can do that. I'm not ready to move on—even if he never loved me.

"Stacia." My voice breaks. "Please tell me where we're going?"

My best friend looks at me with eyes full of sympathy. "You're gonna have to trust me. I *know* you, and I want what's best for you. Please just trust me?"

I shrug and turn back to my reflection.

"AJ, babe, I know this is hard. So, let's make a deal. If you end up hating it, you can shave my head—or wait, I know…you can raid my closet and take anything you want. Seriously, just—trust—me."

For Stacia, those are pretty high stakes, so I decide to follow along.

That is until she drives us to the fucking country club, and I see the huge banner that reads *Congratulations Brock and Amanda* in a sickening powder blue script.

REBEL HEART

CHAPTER TWENTY-FIVE

BROCK

Fuck-a-duck. Getting through the past week has been hell on earth. And that's not an exaggeration. I feel as though I've walked through fire and brimstone, and I damn sure know I've dined with the devil—aka Daddy Dearest. Pretty sure the dude's a full-blown sociopath. Lucky for me, the apple fell *very far* from the tree.

And not banging down Abby Jane's door? Yeah, the struggle was real. I also fought the urge to stalker-call her. Well. I mean, almost. Those first few days weren't so pretty. But Stacia and West helped me get it under control—mostly Stacia after she explained to me that Abby Jane needed space to sort through her emotions. Personally, I thought that was bullshit, because she doesn't have all of the facts. But, whatever. I figured one call a day was plenty of fucking space though. Plus, what if she actually answered?

Now, here I am hoping like hell everything goes according to plan. The sheer number of variables is freaking me the fuck out, though. I need everything to run smoothly. My mom, West, Stacia, and me…we all have a part to play tonight, and if one of them fucks this up, I might explode.

Can't forget the Abby Jane factor, either. That girl doesn't do a damn thing she doesn't want to. *God, please let Stacia get here so I can win her back.* Notice I didn't say *try* to win her back. I'm taking a page from Yoda's playbook: "Do or do not. There is no try." So, fuck yeah, I'm gonna *do*.

I tug at my tie—that not so coincidentally matches the dress Stacia bought my girl—as I step into the room for my sham of an engagement party. It feels like a noose around my neck and as I take in the expertly decorated space, I struggle to breathe.

From the white linen tablecloths and ugly blue runners to the twinkling string lights wound around the vases sitting on every available surface, I can't help but cringe at the wrongness of it all.

While Abby Jane and I weren't anywhere near getting engaged—fucking duh, we hadn't even said the "L" word—I feel like we're headed that way, and I know for sure our party wouldn't be anything like this. Hell. We'd probably go out to Vinny's with West and Stacia and call it a day. That's one of the things I love the most about my girl…how unpretentious she is. My firecracker is down to earth, and real as fuck.

I startle when I feel a strong hand clamp down onto my shoulder. "Son," my dad says. *Should have known it was him.* "I'm so glad you finally came to your senses. I know you think you love that girl, but it'll pass."

REBEL HEART

I shrug out of his hold and offer him a tight-lipped smile.

"Try not to look so angry. You don't want your bride or the guests to think anything's wrong."

My teeth mash together as I restrain myself from saying all of the things I desperately want to say. *In time, Brock. In time. Just be patient.*

I take a deep breath and paste a pleasant smile across my face before turning and walking away without another word. I only have so much willpower.

Ten minutes later, guests begin trickling in, not one of them looking shocked over this impromptu engagement party to a woman I've never even dated. Just goes to show how warped their minds are. None of these people matter, however—there's only one guest I'm interested in, and she's definitely not on the invite list.

Luckily, I don't have to wait long.

My heart stutters in my chest when my eyes land on my girl. Her hair's different, but I fucking love it. It's loud and edgy and sexy—just like her. And Jesus, that dress…it looks like it was made for her and her alone. The look on her face though? It's killing me. She looks absolutely gutted to be here, and that means it's time to get the ball rolling.

ABBY JANE

I'm ready to snap my best friend's neck. I'm not really sure why she thought bringing me here was a good idea, but I'm ready to throw down.

I want to rip down the ugly *Congratulations* banner and burn it on the fucking lawn. I want to pop every single hideous powder blue balloon that's tied to the porch railing. I want to drown Brock and his cunt of a fiancée in the gaudy cake sitting front and center in the entry hall.

I resist the temptation. Not because I care what these people think of me, but because I don't really want to end up in jail, and even more than that, I plan to tell that assholey little weasel exactly what I think to his face.

"Take a breath, AJ," my soon-to-be-former best friend whispers in my ear as we step into the actual party space.

"I fucking hate you." I grit out the words through clenched teeth, yanking my hand from hers, only to stumble back and cling to her when my eyes land on the man of the hour.

Brock's standing in the middle of the room, looking like a dream in his charcoal suit and *dusty rose* tie. *Great…now I'll look like the psycho ex. Maybe I'll wear white to their wedding*—snap out of it! *You will not be attending his wedding!*

He's talking with his and Amanda's parents, while

she clings to him like a damn sloth. A full-body shudder rolls through me, and bile churns in my gut. Brock and I make eye contact, and I turn to flee. Telling him off isn't worth this kind of pain and humiliation.

I don't even make it two steps when Stacia wraps her hand around my wrist, effectively halting my escape. "Sorry, girl. You're just gonna have to trust me."

I glare at her. *Some fucking friend she is.* "Why are you doing this to me?" I ask, my voice cracking with emotion.

"Oh! Look!" she exclaims ignoring the fact that I'm about to break down. "There's West. Let's go say hello."

Stacia sets off, practically dragging me behind her. I dig my heels in, but it doesn't deter her. Not at all.

"Ladies." West tips his head toward us. "How are y'all this fine evening?"

"Nothing fucking fine about it," I mutter under my breath, loud enough for only me to hear.

"We're just waiting for the show," Stacia tells him. They launch into mindless conversation that I promptly tune out—because *fuck this* and *fuck them*. I'd leave, but Stacia's still gripping my wrist like it's a lifeline.

They fall silent when the sound of someone tapping a microphone filters through the speakers hidden around the room. "Looks like it's starting now," West says, rubbing his hands together.

Frustrated to no end, I stomp my foot and ask, "What? What's starting now?"

Stacia shushes me as Mr. Larson begins speaking

into the microphone. Meanwhile, West walks away from us, moving to stand beside Brock.

"Hello and welcome!" His voice booms with manic glee, and a shiver rolls down my spine. "What a momentous occasion. We're here to celebrate the upcoming nuptials between two lovely, upstanding individuals. This day has been a long time coming, and I know I speak for all of us when I say we're honored you're all here!" He raises his glass in the air and the party-goers follow suit.

Fucking gag me with a spoon.

Brock extricates himself from Slut-Manda and steps up to the mic. "Thank you, Dad. And since tonight is, as you said, such a momentous occasion, I've actually prepared a little something for everyone."

CHAPTER TWENTY-SIX

BROCK

I rub my sweaty palms against my slacks and try my hardest not to fidget as two country club employees pull down a large projector screen. After one of the men gives me a thumbs-up, I grab the mic from the podium, suck in a deep breath, and address the crowd.

"You ever have one of those moments that just knocks you on your ass? I'm talking a life-changing, you-know-shit-will-never-be-the-same-again type of moment?

"That's what I had when I first laid eyes on the woman I love. I couldn't have been more than five years old. I remember looking at her and thinking, *I'm gonna marry that girl.* But then, we drifted apart. Well, that's not entirely accurate. I fell victim to preteen hormones and tossed away a treasure. But, my God, when fate placed her in my path again—I was still too stupid and prideful to see what was right in front of me. But I figured it out pretty quickly, and I'm certainly not dumb enough to let her go twice."

I crane my neck and search out Abby Jane in the

crowd. My gaze bores into hers as I try to silently communicate that she's the girl I was talking about. My heart climbs into my chest as Stacia wraps her arms around her, dipping her head to whisper words of comfort in her ear.

I refuse to take my eyes off of Abby Jane as I continue speaking, because really, she's the only one here who matters.

"There's so much in this life we don't get a say in, so much that's beyond our control. On the flip side, there's also a lot that we do get a say in—or at least we should. Things like *what* you spend your life doing, and *who* you do it with. Yet, according to my father, I don't get a say in either."

I can tell dear old dad wants nothing more than to throttle me, but he's too cunning and calculated to make a move in front of everyone. Nah. He much prefers to keep his demons locked behind closed doors.

"I've taken the liberty to prepare a little presentation for y'all. Enjoy." I step to the side and after a bit of static and fuzz, the video begins to play. The room falls silent as everyone watches the events that played out in my father's office last week. The very same events that led to me being here today.

Throughout all of it, I keep my eyes glued to my girl—she looks as nervous as I feel. As the video progresses, I can see the wheels in her mind turning. Every single emotion she's feeling dances across her beautiful features: anger at how my father speaks to

REBEL HEART

me. Outrage and disgust when the truth about my relationship—or lack thereof—with Amanda comes to light. And then hot, molten fury when my father punches me.

When the screen fades to black, I want nothing more than to go to her. Nothing more than to pull her into me and never let go, but I stick to the plan.

Silence blankets the room. That is until Amanda lets out an ear-piercing wail. "Are you shitting me with this?"

Her father tries to silence her, but his fruitless attempt only causes her to turn her anger on him. "You! You promised me I could have him. You lied!"

Fed the fuck up with all of it, I step up to a still-screeching Amanda. "Stop fucking screaming." My voice is low and lethal. "Give me my Mimi's ring and get the hell out of here."

Amanda pries the ring from her finger and chucks it at me. It bounces off of my shoulder and rolls across the floor, where my mother bends and retrieves it.

There's still a lot to hash out, but I have no desire to do it with an audience. Christ knows, we've already given them quite the sideshow act.

I tap on the mic still clutched in my hand and clear my throat. "As y'all can see, there's no cause for celebration here tonight. Sorry for the confusion and the inconvenience. Please pick up your gifts and a slice of cake on the way out."

AJ

The minute people begin filing out of the room, I tuck tail and follow. This night has been one giant clusterfuck of weird, and I need a minute to get my head on straight.

I'm almost home free when Stacia halts my progress. *Again.* "Not so fast, AJ." She directs me back over to where we were standing, positioning between me and the exit so that I can't try and make a break for it. "Are you okay?" she murmurs.

Unsure how to reply, I simply shake my head. So much has happened in such a short window of time, I'm not even sure how to process it.

Brock's dad is a raging, abusive jackass. Amanda is a straight-up sociopath. And Brock…loves me? This night has been like something straight out of a soap opera.

Five minutes later, the only people left in the room are me, Stacia, Brock, West, and Mr. and Mrs. Larson. I notice Brock moving my way, and as if I'm a fucking Olympic sprinter, I rush to close the distance between us.

Brock wastes no time and gathers me into his arms, burying his face in the space between my shoulder and neck. "I'm so sorry, Abby Jane."

REBEL HEART

"Is…is this real?" I whisper brokenly, clinging to him.

"So fucking real. I love you, Abs."

I pull back just enough to peer up at him. "I love you, too."

Our happy reunion is quickly interrupted by none other than his d-bag of a father. "Well, look at the happy couple," he sneers, and Brock whips around to face him, placing himself between us.

"Just give up. It's over. Your bullshit plan failed."

I gasp as he grabs Brock by the collar of his shirt. Just as fast, West moves in to restrain his uncle. As he's hauled away from Brock, he loses his mind. "You ungrateful little shit. Your mother should have fucking aborted you like I fucking told her."

I can tell Brock has something to say, but his mother beats him to it. "That's quite enough, Everett. It seems as though you've forgotten which one of us holds the power."

"You fucking bitch!" he roars, desperately trying to shake West's hold. But Brock's cousin is a beast and only tightens his grip.

"We're finished," Mrs. Larson tells him coolly. "I've had Marta pack you an overnight bag. We'll arrange a date for you to officially move out."

"You can't do this! I won't let you!"

When she simply laughs at his empty threats, he goes berserk, finally breaking free. He charges her and rears back to hit her, but she beats him to the punch—

literally—and rams her knee into his groin, laying him flat out.

She moves to stand over him, a wicked gleam in her eye. "You seem to have forgotten our prenup, Everett. You only get to leave with what you brought into our marriage, and if memory serves…that would be jack shit." She gives him one last repulsed look before spinning on her heel and marching away.

"Come on, kids," she calls over her shoulder, and obediently we all follow behind her leaving Brock's sorry-ass excuse of a father in a heap on the floor.

CHAPTER TWENTY-SEVEN

BROCK

I pull Abby Jane aside while everyone else heads to the parking lot. "Can we go somewhere and talk?" Like the fucking band at Vinny's…seven days without her has made me weak, and I might die if I have to wait another second to have her alone. Plus, we have a fuck-ton to talk about.

She hesitates, and I swear my heart skips a beat… or three. Finally, she nods, and I clasp her hand in mine, leading her to my truck. Stacia shoots us a mischievous grin while West simply smirks.

I pull my keys from my pocket and hit the unlock button before opening Abby Jane's door for her. She's in the process of buckling her seatbelt when my mom walks over and joins us.

Mom wraps me in her arms and squeezes me tight in that way only a mother can. "Oh, honey. I'm so sorry I let things get like this."

"It's okay, Mom."

"No. No, it isn't. But I swear I'll make it up to you. I know you two have a lot to discuss, so go on."

"Are you sure?" I ask, selfishly hoping she says yes so I can get my girl somewhere private.

"I'm sure. Why don't y'all come for breakfast tomorrow?"

I glance to Abby Jane, and she gives a small nod. "Sounds good. Love you."

"Love you too, honey. Drive safe, okay?" Mom presses a kiss to my temple and sets off toward her car.

Abby Jane pulls her door closed, and I head around to the driver's side and climb up next to her. "Mind if we head to your place?" My voice shakes with nerves.

"That's fine, Brock." Her tone is soft and gives nothing away.

The elevator ride up to her apartment is quiet, but not in a comfortable way. It's tense and awkward—much like the drive over. I feel we're trapped in a will-she-or-won't-she limbo.

Will she understand, forgive, and take me back…or will she tell me to kick rocks? Even though she told me she loves me too, I'm still nervous. Is it enough for her to get over what I put her through? Honestly, it could go either way.

Once we enter her apartment, we both just lamely stand there, staring at one another. I'm too chickenshit to make the first move, and Abby Jane looks torn. Finally, after several tense moments, she launches herself at me, twining her arms around my neck and wrapping her legs around my waist.

"Don't think this means you're off the hook." She cries the words against my lips. "I just…need this. Now." Her words end as she licks her tongue across the seam of my lips. Instantly, I part them, granting her entry—like I'd ever deny her.

Our kiss is some sort of reckoning—all-encompassing and powerful. A fucking tornado could have swept us away, and I don't think we would have noticed. She keeps her lips sealed to mine until we have to pull away to breathe.

Both of our chests are heaving as we come back down to earth. "I really fucking love you, firecracker. More than words can describe."

"Speaking of words…I guess we should talk."

"We probably should," I agree.

"C'mon." She links her pinky with mine, not releasing me until we're in her bedroom. "I'm gonna get changed first," she says as I take a seat at the foot of her bed.

Abby Jane turns her back to me and slips the straps of her dress over her shoulders before shimmying it down her body. I almost choke on my fucking tongue when I see that she's as naked as the day she was born.

"Fuuuuuck," I groan out the word, taking in her creamy, tattooed skin, my eyes clinging to the sweet curve of her ass.

The thought of her with nothing under that dress all night just about does me in. She's a temptress without even trying.

She steps into her closet and comes back out in a pair of hipster panties and a tank top and crawls into the bed, slipping under the covers. "Mind if I join?" I ask, not wanting to assume.

"Sure."

"Mind if I get a bit more comfortable?"

She gulps, then shakes her head that she doesn't mind.

Her eyes follow my fingers as I loosen my tie and slip it over my head. Her breath hitches as I undo the buttons of my shirt and remove it. She pulls the duvet up to her chin when I toe off my shoes and socks and remove my pants, leaving me in my boxers.

"Still good?" I ask, not wanting to push her too far out of her comfort zone…yet. Wordlessly, she snakes an arm out from under the covers and pats the spot next to her.

We sit for a few moments, simply staring at one another before she speaks. "I'm not mad at you." She says the words so quietly that I'm not sure if I imagined it or not.

"What?"

"I'm not mad at you." Her voice is stronger now, more confident. "I understand that we were both manipulated and lied to. I know that you tried—many times—to reach out to me. We could have resolved this a while ago if I'd answered your calls, but I…"

"You were hurt," I finish for her. "I don't blame you

for not picking up. I probably wouldn't have either, if our roles were reversed."

"Has…has your dad always been like that?"

"Honestly? Yeah. But it's gotten progressively worse over the years."

I feel her shift under the covers, freezing when I feel her hand brush against my side before she lays it over my heart. "I'm sorry."

"Don't be. Good fucking riddance. Seeing my mom put him in his place tonight was phenomenal."

Abby Jane cracks a small smile. "Yeah, it really was." Slowly, she scoots closer to me, snuggling into my chest. "I do have a question though."

"What's up?"

"Stacia?"

"Ah. Yeah. That was actually all West. The morning after the shitshow at The Colony Grill, while I was at my parents' house, he went to her and explained everything and got her on board. She and I texted all week—she kept me in the loop with how you were, and she helped me plan everything for tonight."

"So that's why your tie matched my dress!" Abby Jane laughs, and it sounds like the best song I've ever heard. "That sneaky, conniving bitch!"

"I'm basically forever indebted to her. But…you're worth it."

"Fuck yeah, I am. Don't you forget it either!"

I roll us so she's flat on her back, with me hovering over her. "Missed that sassy, smart mouth."

"Let's get y'all reacquainted then," she murmurs as she spreads her legs, leaving me room to settle between them.

I grind into her, and she moans. "Missed that too." I practically growl the words as my inner caveman chants *Mine! Mine! Mine!*

She wraps her legs around my waist and uses her toes to push my boxers down. "I want you. I've missed you." She pants the words, and I fucking love it— love that she's just as desperate for me as I am for her.

"Want you too," I groan as I push her panties to the side so I can slide home. "Fuck, Abby Jane, you feel so good. Like heaven."

"Yesss," she hisses as I move inside her, using my body to show her just how sorry I am and how much I love her. "I love you. Don't stop."

"Never, Abs, never." I mean the words in every way imaginable. I'll never stop giving her pleasure. I'll never *not* put her first. I'll never stop loving her. I'll never let her go ever again.

CHAPTER TWENTY-EIGHT

AJ

Brock and I made love on and off all night long, until we were too physically exhausted for more. It seemed like the best idea at the time. But as we drag our tired bodies out of bed to go to his mother's house for breakfast... yeah, not so much.

"C'mon Abs, we gotta get up," Brock murmurs as he drags his fingertips over the dip between my hip bone and rib cage.

"Five more minutes," I beg. "I'm so tired."

He moves his fingers lowers still. "I think we're... what's the equivalent of a sex hangover? Over-orgasmed?"

Chuckling at his antics, I push his hand away and force myself to leave the bed. "I'll start the shower if you start the coffee."

Brock climbs out of the bed, his erection saluting me loud and proud. "Will do, firecracker."

I pad into the bathroom and fiddle with the shower knobs until the temperature is just right. The hot water soothes my aching, well-used muscles. I'm reaching for my shampoo when the door opens and Brock joins me.

"You know," he says as he takes the shampoo bottle from me and squirts some in his palm. "I had an epiphany when I was starting the coffee."

I lean into him as he lathers up my hair, massaging my scalp. "Did you now?"

"I did. You know some people say the only way to cure a hangover is to keep drinking?" I nod and step back under the spray to rinse my hair. "Well, maybe that's the cure for being over-orgasmed…"

"What? Drinking?" I ask, unable to follow his logic.

"No, firecracker." He drops to his knees before me. "More orgasms."

Forty-five minutes and three O's—two for me and one for him—later, we're finally out the door and on our way to breakfast with his mom.

Upside, we're not going to be late. Downside, I'm pretty sure I look exactly how I feel…freshly-fucked. If my rat's nest, semi-damp hair and flushed cheeks aren't a dead giveaway, the lovely hickey I'm sporting on my collarbone will be.

Yay, fun.

Brock picks up on my nervousness as we pull through the massive iron gate that surrounds the Larson house. I jump when I feel his hand come down on my ever-bouncing leg. "Abs, chill. Everything's gonna be fine."

"Is it? What if your dad somehow—"

"That asshole is done. Don't even worry about him, okay?"

I bite the corner of my bottom lip, pulling it into my mouth. "If you say so."

"I do." He parks his truck, and my mind spins at those two little words. *I do*…words he almost gave to someone else. I wonder if one day he'll give them to me? "C'mon, firecracker. Let's go eat."

He grasps my hand as we walk up the steps, only letting go long enough to knock on the door.

"Honey!" his mother exclaims wrapping him in a tight hug. "You don't need to knock. Not anymore."

Brock shrugs his shoulders. "Old habits."

She looks back and forth between the two of us, as if she's not quite sure how to greet me. "Well, y'all come in."

We follow her into the house and the scent of frying bacon fills my nose. "Oh, yum," I groan right as my stomach lets out a loud grumble.

"Smells good, right?" Mrs. Larson asks. "I make sure Marta buys it really fatty. Just tastes better that way."

"That it does," I agree.

We follow her into the kitchen, where there's a kind-looking older woman plating up the most delicious looking breakfast—big, fluffy pancakes dripping with syrup; thick, crisp bacon; and fresh fruit drizzled with poppyseed dressing.

"I thought we could eat on the porch?" Brock's mom asks as she picks up a plate piled high with food. Brock and I do the same and follow her out to the enormous screened-in area.

I'm in the middle of a huge bite when she addresses me. "Abby…AJ…"

"Either," I tell her, covering my mouth with my hand.

"I feel as though I owe you an apology. My husband is a despicable man, and I should have left him long ago. Unfortunately, for a long time, I fed into his *image is everything* diatribe. Thankfully, I've removed my rose-colored glasses. I hate that his actions—our actions—hurt you."

She's definitely right about their actions hurting me, but I can see the genuine remorse in her eyes and hear it in her voice. "It's okay, Mrs. Larson—"

"Please call me Dina, dear."

"It's okay, Dina. I was hurt, but…I get why y'all did it. My parents—as you know—are so much like Mr. Larson. I really just want to put all of it behind us."

"I've always liked you, AJ. I'm very happy you're back in Brock's life. You're good for him." As much as I don't seek approval from others, I beam at her words.

"What about Dad?" Brock asks, addressing the elephant in the room. "What now?"

"I've already met with the lawyer and thanks to our ironclad prenup, it should be a fairly easy process. He'll be by tomorrow to finish packing his things and soon we'll be rid of him altogether."

"I'm proud of you, Mom."

REBEL HEART

"Not as proud as I am of you, honey."

In the weeks after Engagemageddon, Brock and I manage to merge our lives seamlessly. Without the added pressure from his father, he was able to drop his weekend lessons and cut down on his volunteer hours, and he's now working with his advisor on his major.

We still study together twice a week, on Tuesdays and Thursdays. And as of last week, I see him every day, seeing as he moved into my apartment. His reasoning was we had already spent too much time apart—between our lost school-aged years and the week we do our best not to discuss—and to be honest, it was an easy sell.

Especially with finals and graduation looming on the horizon. That shit is sure to keep us busy. Not to mention, falling asleep next to him is no fucking hardship. And waking up to his mouth between my legs is the best alarm clock known to mankind.

EPILOGUE

AJ

A Few Months Later

Within an hour of receiving our diplomas—Brock's in education, not poli-sci, mind you—we were on a private plane—a graduation gift from Brock's mom—Vegas bound. Because what screams *FUCK, YES! WE MADE IT, LET'S CELEBRATE!* louder than the City of Sin? Nothing, that's what.

About an hour into our flight, I'm kicked back in my oversized reclining seat, reading a sexy as sin book about a man falling for his best friend's daughter when Brock whispers huskily in my ear, "Wanna join the Mile High Club, firecracker?" The gravel in his tone, combined with the words on the page in front of me, have me rubbing my thighs together.

"Don't tempt me."

"Why not? It's just us…" His eyes run over my body, lingering heatedly in all the right places.

"And the crew. And the pilot."

"Not if we go to the…fuck, what's the bathroom called on a plane?" He stops and thinks for a moment. "The lavatory! That's it."

I try and hold back my laugh but fail epically. He's so damn cute, and he's all fucking mine. Mine, mine, mine. Some days it doesn't feel real. "Two things, hot shot: One, I'm not fucking you where other people shit. That is nasty. Two, even if I wasn't worried about the nastiness, you killed the mood when you forgot the word."

"You're such a hardass, Abby Jane." He drops into the seat next to me, pouting like a little boy. "Just wanted to spice shit up."

"Oh my God. Stop. Spice things up? You make us sound like an old married couple!"

"Would that be so bad?" he asks. "Being married to me?"

"Wouldn't be bad at all." I pivot in my seat and kick my feet up into his lap. "In fact, I'm setting a deadline. You have a year to propose, Jockstrap. Plan accordingly." Brock makes no effort to reply, but he does begin massaging my feet, so I don't mind.

Before I know it, two and a half hours have passed, and we're getting ready to make our descent. "Mr. Larson, if you and your guest could power down your electronics, stow your personal belongings, move to an upright position and buckle, that would be amazing."

"Can do," Brock tells her, making quick work of following her instructions. Our landing is a little rough, and I grip my man's hand with all of my strength until we're safely taxiing down the runway of the small, private airport.

REBEL HEART

"You ready for an unforgettable trip, Abby Jane?"

"I'm ready for anything with you by my side."

BROCK

After a few hours of sightseeing and doing touristy shit, Abby Jane and I are back at our hotel—the Bellagio—to rest for a few. I have plans for us tonight, and I know my girl gets cranky when she's tired.

"Come lay with me?" Abby Janes asks, stripping out of her clothes and crawling up onto the palatial king-sized bed, knocking the lime green silk pillows off as she goes. The swell of her ass tempts me, and when she flips to her back and spreads her legs, I break.

I'm in the bed and on her faster than I can yell *fore!* I lick, kiss, and bite my way up her smooth, sexy legs until my mouth makes it to the promised land, where I feast on her like a man eating his last meal. By the time I'm finished, my girl's nothing more than a pile of tired limbs.

Her eyelids are drooping and a sated smile paints her lips. *Fuck.* I love seeing her like this—blissed out all because of me. It rattles some primal instinct within me. The same instinct that's insisting I stay in this bed, buried deep inside her.

But…I can't. Because like I said, we've got plans

tonight, and I need to get my ass in gear to lay the groundwork. "I gotta run out really quick, okay? You stay here and take it easy." She manages a small nod, already halfway asleep; I press a soft kiss to her forehead and whisper "I love you" in her ear before getting dressed and walking out the door.

Immediately, I take the elevator down to the lobby and work my way through the massive building to Lago where I make us a reservation for eight o'clock. After that, I make several phone calls, including one to my mother. Luckily, she fully supports my plan. I only have one more errand to run, and it's by far the most important.

I Uber to a well-reputed tattoo shop on the Strip, and after explaining the situation and what I want, they graciously work me in.

I've been gone for over an hour, and I half-expect Abby Jane to be up and waiting on me. But when I step into our gorgeous salon suite, she's still out cold. A quick glance at my watch tells me we have a few hours before we need to be anywhere, so I quickly set an alarm, strip back out of my clothes, and crawl in behind my girl.

An hour later the beeping and buzzing of my phone alarm jolts me awake. "Abs," I murmur against the soft skin of her neck, before giving it a gentle nibble. She moans in her sleep and the sound travels directly to my dick. "Wake up. We gotta get ready."

"Five more minutes," she begs.

"No can do. Gotta get up. I'll go run you a bath."

In the bathroom, I fiddle with the taps until the water is the exact temperature before adding some bath oils. Abby Jane ambles into the room right as I shut off the water. "Good timing." I help her into the tub, marveling at how fucking lucky I am to call her mine.

While Abby Jane lounges in the oversized tub, I shower, shave, and slip into my outfit for the night. Navy slim fit trousers, a crisp white button-down with the top two buttons undone, a matching suit jacket, and a pair of casual brown oxfords. Not gonna lie, I look sharp as fuck.

And judging from my girl's sharp intake of breath when I step back into the bathroom, she agrees.

"Like what you see, firecracker?"

She licks her lips and nods, rising up from the tub, all her slick skin on display. "Very much."

"Play your cards right, and I'll let you strip me out of this suit when we get back to the room tonight."

"That's a promise I'll hold you to, Jockstrap."

"I'm counting on it. Now, get your cute ass ready. We can't be late."

"Where are we going?" she asks, wrapping herself in a plush, white towel.

I give her an innocent shrug. "Can't say."

"Then how do I know what to wear?"

"Dress sexy."

She rolls her pretty brown eyes at me. "You're impossible."

"But you love me!" I wink and head out to the bedroom, plopping down onto the brilliant turquoise sectional.

Thirty minutes later, Abby Jane steps out of the bathroom, wrapped in the hotel robe, with her pastel locks done up in an intricate braid with a few loose tendrils around her face. Her makeup is understated, with a subtle burgundy smoky eye and pale pink lips. She's fucking glowing, and the thought immediately makes me picture her glowing for a different reason—a nine months, congrats-on-your-new-bundle-of-joy kind of reason.

"Since you don't wanna tell me our plans, I don't want you to see my outfit." She flicks her hand at me in a *shooing* motion. "You can go wait in the hall."

"Fair enough, firecracker. Gimme a holler when you're ready." As I walk past her, I make sure my fingers graze her and fuck if I don't love it when she shivers.

Out in the hallway, I mess around on my phone, texting West. After about ten minutes, the room to our door pops open. I step inside, ready to escort my girl downstairs, but instead, my heart stops and my lungs seize. I swear to God, she gets more beautiful to me every day.

But right now, in the moment, she's a fucking vision

REBEL HEART

in white—how ironically appropriate. Her dress is a short little sheath that wraps around her creamy thighs, with cold-shoulders and two sets of straps that crisscross over her chest. She looks so fucking incredible that my eyes don't know where to settle, so they roam her body repeatedly.

She smirks and throws my earlier words back at me. "Like what you see, Jockstrap?"

I advance her, like a predator circling his dinner. "More than you fucking know."

She waltzes past me, smacking my ass as she passes. "C'mon, you said we had plans. Don't wanna be late." *Fucking gorgeous tease.*

AJ

Being in the dark about our plans is killing me. I *know* he has something up his sleeve. I can feel it. I even texted Stacia to snoop for clues, but if she's in the loop, she gave nothing away. *Big shocker there.* She may be my best friend, but she's hardcore Team Brock.

Brock quickly joins me and guides me to the elevator bank with his hand pressed firmly on the small of my back. His fingers twitch against the thin material of my dress. "You okay?"

"Yup. Totally. Wonderful," comes his reply. *Right.*

Because that's not weird. I chalk it up to him being tired since he didn't nap as long as I did.

I let out a little squeal of delight when I realize Brock is taking me to the Conservatory. I know, I know. It doesn't seem like flowers would be my thing…but your ordinary botanical garden, this is not.

"How did you know I would like this?"

"Because I know you, firecracker."

"No. Seriously."

Brock heaves out a fake sigh, pretending to be exasperated with me. "Fine. A little bird named Stacia told me."

"I knew it! Gotta say, you totally fucking nailed it."

We enter through the sky-high Torii Gates, and, I kid you not, it's like stepping into a fairy realm. Brock is as enchanted as I am by the out of this world floral and botanical displays—from the blooming cherry blossoms and lotus flowers to the peaceful waterfalls and the massive, twenty-six feet tall, floral woman rising up from the water.

There are so many over the top features that I don't know where to look next. By the time we finish our tour, I'm absolutely blown away—almost to the point of tears—by the intricate beauty.

"That was perfect," I say, sidling up next to Brock so that my head rests on his shoulder. "Wanna grab dinner now or later?"

"Now," he says with a slight tremor to his voice. He leads me through the lobby and into Lago—a highly praised Italian restaurant.

Brock seems distracted as we wait for our food to arrive. He's tapping his foot, twiddling his thumbs while staring at his lap, and I'm pretty sure there's a fine sheen of sweat dotting his hairline, even though it's pretty damn chilly in here.

"Are you sure you're okay?"

He glances up at me and offers a small smile. "Totally."

"Well, you're acting a little nutso, so you'll have to excuse me for not buying what you're selling, Jockstrap."

"Sorry. I guess I'm just tired."

He doesn't sound tired, but I decide to take him at his word. "Well, we don't have to go out tonight. We have all week."

He's about to reply when our server comes out with our meals. In lieu of entrees, we decide to split several small plates—including short rib, filet, bruschetta, and mushroom risotto—and each one is more delicious than the last.

We've just placed our dessert order when Brock clears his throat, pulling my attention away from the glorious fountain show.

"So," he taps his fingers on the tabletop. "What you said earlier got me thinking."

"What I said about what?" I ask, confused because let's be real…I talk…*a lot.*

"About getting married."

"What about it?" I laugh at how adorably awkward

he's being. "Use your big boy words."

"It's just...I love you. And hell, I've already announced to practically *everyone* we know that I've been crushin' on you since like kindergarten. And God, Abs, those years when you weren't in my life...there wasn't a single day that went by where I didn't think of you. When I didn't regret ruining our friendship because I was a horny little preteen asswipe."

His tone is serious, and his words hit me right in the feels. "That's all in the past. We made it. And we're gonna keep on making it. You don't have to keep appologiz—"

He cuts me off. "I'm not apologizing. It's just... you're *it* for me. When I saw you in the library that day and learned you were my tutor, it was like the fucking clouds parted for the first time in a long time."

"Look at you, being all sentimental. You're def getting some tonight."

He shoots me a sexy smirk but doesn't otherwise acknowledge what I said. "I know we're young, Abby Jane, but I don't want to wait a year to propose. I know this seems spur of the moment, but I've actually had this ring for a couple of weeks now. And after everything that's happened between us, I've learned waiting for the perfect moment can bite you in the ass."

"Wh-what are you saying?" I blink at him like a deer in headlights. Surely, he's not...

He pushes his chair back from the table and drops to one knee. Reading my panicked expression, he rushes on. "Hear me out. I already know you're my future—my forever…" He fishes around in his pocket, retrieving a black velvet box, flipping it open to reveal the most breathtaking emerald-cut smoky quartz ring. The stone is nestled in a diamond halo and set in a rose gold band.

"…I love you, firecracker. Marry me? Please?"

"Yes!" I launch myself into his arms. "Yes!"

"Yes?" he asks, almost disbelievingly.

"God! YES, you dumbass! How could you possibly think I'd say no?"

"I learned a long time ago not to assume with you."

"Riiiight. You know I'm a sure thing. Hell. I pretty much demanded you ask me earlier today. You just sped up the timeline. I love you, Jockstrap, and there's no one else out there for me."

"Damn straight. There's definitely no one else who could put up with your ass."

"Asshole," I say on a laugh, right as our dessert is placed on the table before us. But we're too into each other—into this moment—to bother eating it. I stare at the ring on my finger, admiring how it glows in the low lights.

"Abs!" Brock practically shouts my name.

I jerk my head up at the tone of his voice. "Gah! What?"

"You know I said your name like three times, right?"

I bite my lip and shake my head. "No, sorry. I was too busy ogling my ring."

"I'm glad you like it. But, I…I have another

question."

I wink at him. "If you're about to ask me to have your baby, the answer is no."

"Jesus, you're impossible. No…I wanted…well, the thing is, I want to marry you now. Hell, you're already wearing white."

"Hold up. I'm not saying my vows in front of an Elvis impersonator."

"No worries. I have it covered."

I wait for our server to drop off our check before speaking. But as soon as she's gone… "Excuse me! What exactly do you mean you've *got it covered*? This is our wedding. Our one and only wedding and I know I'm not like most girls, but I've still imagined that my big day would be like. Not to mention, our families, what about them?"

Brock raises a brow at me. "Okay, sure, the only family involved is your mother. But I bet she would like to be here. And West and Stacia—what about them?"

"Calm down. I want you to trust me. Can you do that?"

"Of course, I trust you, Brock. But…now?"

"I can't wait another second to call you my wife. For you to have my last name. And let's be real, a big to-do wedding is so not your thing."

I place my palms on the table and stare him down. "You think you know me so well…"

"I know I do. If I had to wager a guess, I'd say you'd rather elope than drop buckets of money that could be put toward something else—like our future together."

I let out a small growl, because *dammit*, he's right. But even still, I always pictured Stacia by my side.

After paying our tab, Brock suggests checking out the fountains from the terrace. I easily agree because they're beautiful. Plus, maybe we can snap a *just engaged* picture to send Stacia.

Except, when we get out there, Brock turns to me and asks me to give him a few minutes.

"What? Right now? Seriously?"

He boops me on the nose, and I smack his hand away. "I said to trust me." He grins and spins on his heels, walking over to a gentleman who appears to have been expecting our arrival.

The two of them talk for a minute before gesturing for me to join them. Even though I'm confused as fuck, my feet move me toward him.

"Ready to say 'I do,' firecracker?" Brock asks, his tone a mixture of sheepish and excited.

"Here?" I ask. I'm equal parts elated and melancholy. Because while this is a stunning venue, it doesn't feel right without my bestie.

"Yeah, baby, here." He nods and I see Stacia, West, and his mom step around a group of people.

My best friend squeals and tackle-hugs me—thankfully Brock was right behind me and kept us upright. "OMG! You're getting married!"

My eyes gloss over with tears. "I am! Wait, how are you here?" I dumbly ask.

She tips her head to my fiancé. I spin to face him. "Y-you planned this? While I slept?" He nods. "Then let's fucking get married!"

"Way to set the bar high, cousin," West growls, patting him on the back as we take our places.

"You heard the lady," Brock says to the officiant.

"Brock and Abigail, please join hands." We do. "Brock, please repeat after me—"

Brock cuts him off. "Actually, I've prepared my own vows, if that's okay?" Our officiant nods. "Abby Jane, you're the best thing in my life. You're my wild, and I can't imagine my life without you in it. You're my light when it's dark. My saving grace. Everything is better with you by my side, and I can't fucking imagine spending my life with anyone but you. I promise to love you through it all—good and bad—always."

Big, happy tears roll down my cheeks, probably ruining my makeup, but I don't have it in me to care. "Do you have your own vows prepared?" the officiant asks me.

I snort out a wobbly laugh. "Nope. I'm gonna wing it. Brock Larson, you're one of the most infuriating, most impossible men I've ever met. You challenge me every day to be my best self, and you keep me grounded. You're my rock, and I can't wait to grow old with you. And so help me God, you better still love me when my tattoos are so wrinkly you can't tell what they are anymore."

This time it's Brock who's laughing.

REBEL HEART

"Brock, do you take Abigail to be your wife?"

"Hell yes," my groom murmurs.

"Abigail, do you take Brock to be your husband?"

"Fuck. Yes."

Our officiant smirks and continues. "Please present the rings."

"Wait!" I exclaim. "I don't have a ring for you, Brock!"

"No worries, firecracker. I took care of it." He peels back the little Band-Aid that slipped my notice, revealing a little firecracker tattooed on his ring finger.

My eyes widen and my heart races. "You did that for me?" I whisper.

"Don't you know I'll do anything for you?" He reaches out and wipes my tears away.

Once my ring is blessed, we move on to the good part. "You may now kiss your bride."

I wrap my arms around Brock's neck, and he dips me low, claiming my lips with his, and all I can think is…if this is what forever feels like, sign me the fuck up.

THE END

ACKNOWLEDGEMENTS

To my testes…they say the triangle is the strongest shape and nature, and with y'all by my side, I know that shit's true.

Lo, you get me like no other. You're my soul sister from another mother and another mister. I abso-fucking-lutely adore you and value your friendship like you couldn't believe. Love you forever and then some. #Tripod4Life

Heather, gah! How lame would my life be without you? LAME AF. You're hands down one of the most real and selfless people I know. You're an angel with the mouth of a sailor and I'm proud to call you my friend. #Tripod4life

Joy, I'm so glad we're friends. I can always count on you to be real with me and I love bouncing ideas around with you.

Jodie, I absolutely adore you. Our talks always make me smile. <3

Dani, guuuuurl. To the moon and back, okay? Seriously, you're my boo thang and I lurve you.

Jennifer Van Wyk, you make my soul happy. You're such a light and I'm so glad to have you in my life.

Kiezha, as always, your edits are on point.

Ellie McLove, I'm so damn thrilled to have you on my team. Your edits are so much yes.

Jules, you always manage to dish up the most perfect covers. Thank you for your patience with me. And thank you so much for being there for me when I really needed someone. It means the world to me.

Megan and Harloe, you ladies are everything good and right in this world and I'm blessed to count y'all as friends.

To my betas: Allyson, Dani, Hopey, Joy, & Kaffy… thank you ladies for being the very first eyes on Brock and AJ. You support, eagle eyes, and sharp minds means the world to me.

To all my DND babes, <3

And most of all, to the bloggers and readers who pick up my books…THANK YOU! SERIOUSLY, THANK YOU! Your support is everything to me.

ABOUT THE AUTHOR

LK Farlow (A.K.A Kate) is a small town girl with a love for words. She's been writing stories and poems for as long she can remember. A Southern girl through and through, Kate resides in beautiful, sunny LA—that's Lower Alabama, y'all—with her amazing husband and three wonderful children. When she's not writing, you can find her snuggled up on the couch watching nature documentaries while she crochets or with her nose in a book. All Kate really wants in this life is her family happy, strong coffee, a good book and more Happily Ever After's

Facebook, Twitter, & Insta: @AuthorLKFarlow
Reader Group: LK's Darling's
www.authorlkfarlow.com

Made in the USA
Columbia, SC
24 December 2018

Made in the USA
Charleston, SC
11 July 2010